Book Four

Winter

The Lunar Chronicles

WRITTEN BY

Marissa Meyer

Feiwel and Friends
NEW YORK

A FEIWEL AND FRIENDS BOOK
An Imprint of Macmillan

Our books may be purchased in bulk for promotional, educational, or business
use. Please contact your local bookseller or the Macmillan Corporate and
Premium Sales Department at (800) 221-7945 ext. 5442 or by e-mail at
MacmillanSpecialMarkets@macmillan.com.

Library of Congress Cataloging-in-Publication Data Available

ISBN
978-0-312-64298-3 (hardcover)
978-1-250-07421-8 (international edition)
978-1-250-06875-0 (ebook)

Feiwel and Friends logo designed by Filomena Tuosto

First Edition: 2015

10 9 8 7 6 5 4 3 2 1

macteenbooks.com

*For Jesse, who turns every day
into a happily ever after.*

BOOK
One

The young princess was as beautiful

as daylight. She was more beautiful even

than the queen herself.

One

WINTER'S TOES HAD BECOME ICE CUBES. THEY WERE AS COLD as space. As cold as the dark side of Luna. As cold as—

"...security feeds captured him entering the AR-Central med-clinic's sublevels at 23:00 U.T.C...."

Thaumaturge Aimery Park spoke with a serene, measured cadence, like a ballad. It was easy to lose track of what he was saying, easy to let all the words blur and conjoin. Winter curled her toes inside her thin-soled shoes, afraid that if they got any colder before this trial was over, they would snap off.

"...was attempting to interfere with one of the shells currently stored..."

Snap off. One by one.

"...records indicate the shell child is the accused's son, taken on 29 July of last year. He is now fifteen months old."

Winter hid her hands in the folds of her gown. They were shaking again. She was always shaking these days. She squeezed her fingers to hold them still and pressed the bottoms of her feet into the hard floor. She struggled to bring the throne room into focus before it dissolved.

The throne room, in the central tower of the palace, had the most striking view in the city. From her seat, Winter could see Artemisia Lake mirroring the white palace and the city reaching for the edge of the enormous clear dome that sheltered them from the outside elements—or lack thereof. The throne room itself extended past the walls of the tower, so that when one passed beyond the edge of the mosaic floor, they found themselves on a ledge of clear glass. Like standing on air, about to plummet into the depths of the crater lake.

To Winter's left she could make out the edges of her stepmother's fingernails as they dug into the arm of her throne, an imposing seat carved from white stone. Normally her stepmother was calm during these proceedings and would listen to the trials without a hint of emotion. Winter was used to seeing Levana's fingertips stroking the polished stone, not throttling it. But tension was high since Levana and her entourage had returned from Earth, and her stepmother had flown into even more rages than usual these past months.

Ever since that runaway Lunar—that *cyborg*—had escaped from her Earthen prison.

Ever since war had begun between Earth and Luna.

Ever since the queen's betrothed had been kidnapped, and Levana's chance to be crowned empress had been stolen from her.

The blue planet hung above the horizon, cut clean in half. Luna was a little more than halfway through the long night, and the city of Artemisia glowed with pale blue lampposts and glowing crystal windows, their reflections dancing across the lake's surface.

Winter missed the sun and its warmth. Their artificial days were never the same.

"How did he know about the shells?" Queen Levana asked. "Why did he not believe his son to have been killed at birth?"

Seated around the room in four tiered rows were the families. The queen's court. The nobles of Luna, granted favor with Her Majesty for their generations of loyalty, their extraordinary talents with the Lunar gift, or pure luck at having been born a citizen of the great city of Artemisia.

Then there was the man on his knees beside Thaumaturge Park. He had not been born lucky.

His hands were together, pleading. Winter wished she could tell him it wouldn't matter. All his begging would be for nothing. She thought there would be comfort in knowing there was nothing you could do to avoid death. Those who came before the queen having already accepted their fate seemed to have an easier time of it.

She looked down at her own hands, still clawed around her gauzy white skirt. Her fingers had been bitten with frost. It was sort of pretty. Glistening and shimmering and *cold, so very cold*...

"Your queen asked you a question," said Aimery.

Winter flinched, as if he'd been yelling at her.

Focus. She must try to focus.

She lifted her head and inhaled.

Aimery was wearing white now, having replaced Sybil Mira as the queen's head thaumaturge. The gold embroidery on his coat shimmered as he circled the captive.

"I am sorry, Your Majesty," the man said. "My family and I have served you for generations. I'm a janitor at that med-clinic and I'd heard rumors . . . It was none of my business, so I never cared, I never listened. But . . . when my son was born a shell . . ." He whimpered. "He is my *son*."

"Did you not think," said Levana, her voice loud and crisp,

"there might be a reason your queen has chosen to keep your son and all the other ungifted Lunars separate from our citizens? That we may have a purpose that serves the good of *all* our people by containing them as we have?"

The man gulped hard enough that Winter could see his Adam's apple bobbing. "I know, My Queen. I know you use their blood for . . . experimentation. But . . . but you have *so many*, and he's only a baby, and . . ."

"Not only is his blood valuable to the success of our political alliances, the likes of which I cannot expect a janitor from the outer sectors to understand, but he is also a shell, and his kind have proven themselves to be dangerous and untrustworthy, as you will recall from the assassinations of King Marrok and Queen Jannali eighteen years ago. Yet you would subject our society to this threat?"

The man's eyes were wild with fear. "Threat, My Queen? He is a *baby*." He paused. He did not look outright rebellious, but his lack of remorse would be sending Levana into a fury soon enough. "And the others in those tanks . . . so many of them, children. Innocent *children*."

The room chilled.

He knew too much. The shell infanticide had been in place since the rule of Levana's sister, Queen Channary, after a shell sneaked into the palace and killed their parents. No one would be pleased to know their babies had not been killed at all, but instead locked away and used as tiny blood-platelet-manufacturing plants.

Winter blinked, imagining her own body as a blood-platelet-manufacturing plant.

Her gaze dropped again. The ice had extended to her wrists now.

That would not be beneficial for the platelet conveyor belts.

"Does the accused have a family?" asked the queen.

Aimery bobbed his head. "Records indicate a daughter, age nine. He also has two sisters and a nephew. All live in Sector GM-12."

"No wife?"

"Dead five months past of regolith poisoning."

The prisoner watched the queen, desperation pooling around his knees.

The court began to stir, their vibrant clothes fluttering. This trial had gone on too long. They were growing bored.

Levana leaned against the back of her throne. "You are hereby found guilty of trespassing and attempted theft against the crown. This crime is punishable by immediate death."

The man shuddered, but his face remained pleading. It always took them a few seconds to comprehend such a sentence.

"Your family members will each receive a dozen public lashings as a reminder to your sector that I do not tolerate my decisions being questioned."

The man's jaw slackened.

"Your daughter will be given as a gift to one of the court's families. There, she will be taught the obedience and humility one can assume she has not learned beneath your tutelage."

"No, please. Let her live with her aunts. She hasn't done anything!"

"Aimery, you may proceed."

"*Please!*"

"Your queen has spoken," said Thaumaturge Aimery. "Her word is final."

Aimery drew an obsidian knife from one of his bell-shaped

sleeves and held the handle toward the prisoner, whose eyes had gone wide with hysteria.

The room grew colder. Winter's breath crystallized in the air. She squeezed her arms tight against her body.

The prisoner took the knife handle. His hand was steady. The rest of him was trembling.

"Please. My little girl—I'm all she has. *Please.* My Queen. Your Majesty!"

He raised the blade to his throat.

This was when Winter looked away. When she always looked away. She watched her own fingers burrow into her dress, her fingernails scraping at the fabric until she could feel the sting on her thighs. She watched the ice climb over her wrists, toward her elbows. Where the ice touched, her flesh went numb.

She imagined lashing out at the queen with those ice-solid fists. She imagined her hands shattering into a thousand icicle shards.

It was at her shoulders now. Her neck.

Even over the popping and cracking of the ice, she heard the cut of flesh. The burble of blood and a muffled gag. The hard slump of the body.

The cold had stolen into her chest. She squeezed her eyes shut, reminding herself to be calm, to breathe. She could hear Jacin's steady voice in her head, his hands gripping her shoulders. *It isn't real, Princess. It's only an illusion.*

Usually they helped, these memories of him coaxing her through the panic. But this time it seemed to prompt the ice on. Encompassing her rib cage. Gnawing into her stomach. Hardening over her heart.

She was freezing from the inside out.

Listen to my voice.

Jacin wasn't there.

Stay with me.

Jacin was gone.

It's all in your head.

She heard the clomping of the guards' boots as they approached the body. The corpse being slid toward the ledge. The shove and the distant splash below.

The court applauded with quiet politeness.

Winter heard her toes snap off. One. By. One.

"Very good," said Queen Levana. "Thaumaturge Tavaler, see to it that the rest of the sentencing is carried out."

The ice was in her throat now, climbing up her jaw. There were tears freezing inside their ducts. There was saliva crystallizing on her tongue.

She raised her head as a servant began washing the blood from the tiles. Aimery, rubbing his knife with a cloth, met Winter's gaze. His smile was searing. "I am afraid the princess has no stomach for these proceedings."

The nobles in the audience tittered—Winter's disgust of the trials was a source of merriment to most of Levana's court.

The queen turned, but Winter couldn't look up. She was a girl made of ice and glass. Her teeth were brittle, her lungs too easily shattered.

"Yes," said Levana. "I often forget she's here at all. You're about as useless as a rag doll, aren't you, Winter?"

The audience chuckled again, louder now, as if the queen had given permission to mock the young princess. But Winter couldn't respond, not to the queen, not to the laughter. She kept her focus on the thaumaturge, trying to hide her panic.

"Oh, no, she isn't quite as useless as that," Aimery said. As Winter stared, a thin crimson line drew itself across his throat, blood bubbling up from the wound. "The prettiest girl on all of Luna? She will make some member of this court a happy bride someday, I should think."

"The prettiest girl, Aimery?" Levana's light tone almost concealed the snarl beneath.

Aimery slipped into a bow. "Prettiest only, My Queen. But no mortal could compare with your perfection."

The court was quick to agree, offering a hundred compliments at once, though Winter still felt the leering gazes of more than one noble attached to her.

Aimery took a step toward the throne and his severed head tipped off, thunking against the marble and rolling, rolling, rolling, until it stopped at Winter's frozen feet.

Still smiling.

She whimpered, but the sound was buried beneath the snow in her throat.

It's all in your head.

"Silence," said Levana, once she'd had her share of praise. "Are we finished?"

Finally, the ice found her eyes and Winter had no choice but to shut them against Aimery's headless apparition, enclosing herself in cold and darkness.

She would die here and not complain. She would be buried beneath this avalanche of lifelessness. She would never have to witness another murder again.

"There is one more prisoner still to be tried, My Queen." Aimery's voice echoed in the cold hollowness of Winter's head. "Sir Jacin Clay, royal guard, pilot, and assigned protector of Thaumaturge Sybil Mira."

Winter gasped and the ice shattered, a million sharp glittering bits exploding across the throne room and skidding across the floor. No one else heard them. No one else noticed.

Aimery, head very much attached, was watching her again, as if he'd been waiting to see her reaction. His smirk was subtle as he returned his attention to the queen.

"Ah, yes," said Levana. "Bring him in."

Two

THE DOORS TO THE THRONE ROOM OPENED, AND THERE HE was, trapped between two guards, his wrists corded behind his back. His blond hair was clumped and matted, strands of it clinging to his jaw. It appeared to have been a fair while since he'd last showered, but Winter could detect no obvious signs of abuse.

Her stomach flipped. All the warmth the ice had sucked out of her came rushing back to the surface of her skin.

Stay with me, Princess. Listen to my voice, Princess.

He was led to the center of the room, devoid of expression. Winter jabbed her fingernails into her palms.

Jacin didn't look at her. Not once.

"Jacin Clay," said Aimery, "you have been charged with betraying the crown by failing to protect Thaumaturge Mira and by failing to apprehend a known Lunar fugitive despite nearly two weeks spent in said fugitive's company. You are a traitor to Luna and to our queen. These crimes are punishable by death. What have you to say in your defense?"

Winter's heart thundered like a drum against her ribs. She

turned pleading eyes up to her stepmother, but Levana was not paying her any attention.

"I plead guilty to all stated crimes," said Jacin, drawing Winter's attention back, "*except* for the accusation that I am a traitor."

Levana's fingernails fluttered against the arm of her throne. "Explain."

Jacin stood as tall and stalwart as if he were in uniform, as if he were on duty, not on trial. "As I've said before, I did not apprehend the fugitive while in her company because I was attempting to convince her I could be trusted, in order to gather information for my queen."

"Ah, yes, you were spying on her and her companions," said Levana. "I do recall that excuse from when you were captured. I also recall that you had no pertinent information to give me, only lies."

"Not lies, My Queen, though I will admit I underestimated the cyborg and her abilities. She was disguising them from me."

"So much for earning her trust." There was mocking in the queen's tone.

"Knowledge of the cyborg's skills was not the only information I sought, My Queen."

"I suggest you stop playing with words. My patience with you is already thin."

Winter's heart shriveled. Not Jacin. She could not sit here and watch them kill Jacin.

She would bargain for him, she decided, though the plan came with a flaw. What did she have to bargain with? Nothing but her own life, and Levana would not accept that.

She could throw a fit. Go into hysterics. It would hardly be a stretch from the truth at this point, and it might distract them for a time, but it would only delay the inevitable.

She had felt helpless many times in her life, but never like this.

Only one thing to be done, then. She would throw her own body in front of the blade.

Oh, Jacin would *hate* that.

Ignorant of Winter's newest resolve, Jacin respectfully inclined his head. "During my time with Linh Cinder, I uncovered information about a device that can nullify the effects of the Lunar gift when connected to a person's nervous system."

This caused a curious squirm through the crowd. A stiffening of spines, a tilting forward of shoulders.

"Impossible," said Levana.

"Linh Cinder had evidence of its potential. As it was described to me, on an Earthen, the device will keep their bioelectricity from being tampered with. But on a Lunar, it will prevent them from using their gift at all. Linh Cinder herself had the device installed when she arrived at the Commonwealth ball. Only when it was destroyed was she able to use her gift—as was evidenced with your own eyes, My Queen."

His words carried an air of impertinence. Levana's knuckles turned white.

"How many of these hypothetical devices exist?"

"To my knowledge, only the broken device installed in the cyborg herself. But I suspect there still exist patents or blueprints. The inventor was Linh Cinder's adoptive father."

The queen's grip began to relax. "This is intriguing information, Sir Clay. But it speaks more of a desperate attempt to save yourself than true innocence."

Jacin shrugged, nonchalant. "If my loyalty cannot be seen in how I conducted myself with the enemy, obtaining this information and alerting Thaumaturge Mira to the plot to kidnap Emperor Kaito, I don't know what other evidence I can provide for you, My Queen."

"Yes, yes, the anonymous tip Sybil received, alerting her to Linh Cinder's plans." Levana sighed. "I find it very convenient that this comm you *claim* to have sent was seen by no one other than Sybil herself, who is now dead."

For the first time, Jacin looked off balance beneath the queen's glare. He still had not looked at Winter.

The queen turned to Jerrico Solis, her captain of the guard. Like so many of the queen's guards, Jerrico made Winter uncomfortable, and she often had visions of his orange-red hair going up in flames and the rest of him burning down to a smoldering coal. "You were with Sybil when she ambushed the enemy's ship that day, yet you said before that Sybil had mentioned no such comm. Have you anything to add?"

Jerrico took a step forward. He had returned from their Earthen excursion with a fair share of bruises, but they had begun to fade. "My Queen, Thaumaturge Mira seemed confident we would find Linh Cinder on that rooftop, but she did not mention receiving any outside information—anonymous or otherwise. When the ship landed, it was Thaumaturge Mira who ordered Jacin Clay to be taken into custody."

Jacin's eyebrow twitched. "Perhaps she was still upset that I shot her." He paused, before adding, "While under Linh Cinder's control, in my defense."

"You seem to have plenty to say in your defense," said Levana.

Jacin didn't respond. It was the calmest Winter had ever seen a prisoner—he, who knew better than anyone the horrible things that happened on this floor, in the very spot where he stood. Levana should have been infuriated by his audacity, but she seemed merely thoughtful.

"Permission to speak, My Queen?"

The crowd rustled and it took a moment for Winter to discern who had spoken. It was a *guard.* One of the silent ornamentations of the palace. Though she recognized him, she didn't know his name.

Levana glowered at him, and Winter imagined her calculating whether to grant the permission or punish the man for speaking out of turn. Finally, she said, "What is your name, and why do you dare interrupt these proceedings?"

The guard stepped forward, staring at the wall, always at the wall. "My name is Liam Kinney, My Queen. I assisted with the retrieval of Thaumaturge Mira's body."

A questioning eyebrow to Jerrico; a confirming nod received. "Go on," said Levana.

"Mistress Mira was in possession of a portscreen when we found her, and though it was broken in the fall, it was still submitted as evidence in the case of her murder. I wonder if anyone has attempted to retrieve the alleged comm."

Levana turned her attention back to Aimery, whose face was a mask that Winter recognized. The more pleasant his expression, the more annoyed he was. "In fact, we did manage to access her recent communications. I was about to bring forward the evidence."

It was a lie, which gave Winter hope. Aimery was a great liar, especially when it was in his best interests. And he hated Jacin. He would not want to give up anything that could help him.

Hope. Frail, flimsy, pathetic *hope.*

Aimery gestured toward the door and a servant scurried

forward, carrying a shattered portscreen and a holograph node on a tray. "This is the portscreen Sir Kinney mentioned. Our investigation has confirmed that there was, indeed, an anonymous comm sent to Sybil Mira that day."

The servant turned on the node and a holograph shimmered into the center of the room—behind it, Jacin faded away like a phantom.

The holograph displayed a basic text comm.

Linh Cinder plotting to kidnap EC emperor.
Escape planned from north tower rooftop, sunset.

So much importance pressed into so few words. It was just like Jacin.

Levana read the words with narrowed eyes. "Thank you, Sir Kinney, for bringing this to our attention." It was telling that she did not thank Aimery.

The guard, Kinney, bowed and stepped back into position. His gaze flickered once to Winter, unreadable, before attaching again to the far wall.

Levana continued, "I suppose you will tell me, Sir Clay, that this was the comm you sent."

"It was."

"Have you anything else to add before I make my verdict?"

"Nothing, My Queen."

Levana leaned back in her throne and the room hushed, everyone awaiting the queen's decision.

"I trust my stepdaughter would like me to spare you."

Jacin didn't react, but Winter winced at the haughtiness in her stepmother's tone. "Please, Stepmother," she whispered, the words clumping on her dry tongue. "It's *Jacin*. He is not our enemy."

"Not *yours*, perhaps," Levana said. "But you are a naïve, stupid girl."

"That is not so. I am a factory for blood and platelets, and all my machinery is freezing over . . ."

The court burst into laughter, and Winter recoiled. Even Levana's lips twitched, though there was annoyance beneath her amusement.

"I have made my decision," she said, her booming voice demanding silence. "I have decided to let the prisoner live."

Winter released a cry of relief. She clapped a hand over her mouth, but it was too late to stifle the noise.

There were more giggles from the audience.

"Have you any other insights to add, Princess?" Levana said through her teeth.

Winter gathered her emotions as well as she could. "No, My Queen. Your rulings are always wise and final, My Queen."

"This ruling is not finished." The queen's voice hardened as she addressed Jacin again. "Your inability to kill or capture Linh Cinder will not go unpunished, as your incompetence led to her successful kidnapping of my betrothed. For this crime, I sentence you to thirty self-inflicted lashings to be held on the central dais, followed by forty hours of penance. Your sentence shall commence at tomorrow's light-break."

Winter flinched, but even this punishment could not destroy the fluttery relief in her stomach. He was not going to die. She was not a girl of ice and glass at all, but a girl of sunshine and stardust, because Jacin wasn't going to die.

"And, Winter . . ."

She jerked her attention back to her stepmother, who was eyeing her with disdain. "If you attempt to bring him food, I will have his tongue removed in payment for your kindness."

She shrank back into her chair, a tiny ray of her sunshine extinguished. "Yes, My Queen."

Three

WINTER WAS AWAKE HOURS BEFORE LIGHT BRIGHTENED THE
dome's artificial sky, having hardly slept. She did not go to
watch Jacin receive his lashings, knowing that if he saw her, he
would have kept himself from screaming in pain. She wouldn't
do that to him. Let him scream. He was still stronger than any
of them.

She dutifully nibbled at the cured meats and cheeses brought
for her breakfast. She allowed the servants to bathe her and
dress her in pale pink silk. She sat through an entire session
with Master Gertman, a third-tier thaumaturge and her long-
standing tutor, pretending to try to use her gift and apologizing
when it was too hard, when she was too weak. He did not seem
to mind. Anyway, he spent most of their sessions gazing slack-
jawed at her face, and Winter didn't know if he would be able to
tell if she really did glamour him for once.

The artificial day had come and gone; one of the maidser-
vants had brought her a mug of warmed milk and cinnamon and
turned down her bed, and finally Winter was left alone.

Her heart pounded with anticipation.

She slipped into a pair of lightweight linen pants and a loose top, then pulled on her night robe so it would look like she was wearing her bedclothes underneath. She had thought of this all day, the plan taking form in her mind, like tiny puzzle pieces snapping together. Willful determination had stifled any hallucinations.

She fluffed her hair to look as if she'd woken from a deep slumber, turned off the lights, and climbed up onto her bed. The dangling chandelier clipped her brow and she flinched, stepping back and catching her balance on the thick mattress.

Winter braced herself with a breath full of intentions.

Counted to three.

And screamed.

She screamed like an assassin was driving a knife into her stomach.

She screamed like a thousand birds were pecking at her flesh.

She screamed like the palace was burning down around her.

The guard stationed outside her door burst inside, weapon drawn. Winter went on screaming. Stumbling back over her pillows, she pressed her back against the headboard and clawed at her hair.

"Princess! What is it? What's wrong?" His eyes darted around the dark room, searching for an intruder, a threat.

Flailing an arm behind her, Winter scratched at the wallpaper, tearing off a shred. It was becoming easier to believe she was horrified. There were phantoms and murderers closing in around her.

"Princess!" A second guard burst into the room. He flipped on the light and Winter ducked away from it. "What's going on?"

"I don't know." The first guard had crossed to the other side of the room and was checking behind the window drapes.

"*Monster!*" Winter shrieked, bulleting the statement with a sob. "I woke up and he was standing over my bed—one of—one of the queen's soldiers!"

The guards traded looks and the silent message was clear, even to Winter.

Nothing's wrong. She's just crazy.

"Your Highness—" started the second guard, as a third appeared at the doorway.

Good. There were only three guards regularly stationed in this corridor between her bedroom and the main stairway.

"He went that way!" Cowering behind one arm, Winter pointed toward her dressing closet. "Please. Please don't let him get away. Please find him!"

"What's happened?" asked the newcomer.

"She thinks she saw one of the mutant soldiers," grumbled the second guard.

"*He was here,*" she screamed, the words tearing at her throat. "Why aren't you protecting me? Why are you standing there? *Go find him!*"

The first guard looked annoyed, as if this charade had interrupted something more than standing in the hallway and staring at a wall. He holstered his gun, but said, with authority, "Of course, Princess. We will find this perpetrator and ensure your safety." He beckoned the second guard and the two of them stalked off toward the closet.

Winter turned to the third guard and fell into a crouch. "You must go with them," she urged, her voice fluttery and weak. "He is a monster—enormous—with ferocious teeth and claws that will tear them to *shreds*. They can't defeat him alone, and if they fail—!" Her words turned into a wail of terror. "He'll come for me, and there will be no one to stop him. No one will save me!" She pulled at her hair, her entire body quivering.

"All right, all right. Of course, Highness. Just wait here, and . . . try to calm yourself." Looking grateful to leave the mad princess behind, he took off after his comrades.

No sooner had he disappeared did Winter slip off the bed and shrug out of her robe, leaving it draped over a chair.

"The closet is clear!" one of the guards yelled.

"Keep looking!" she yelled back. "I know he's in there!"

Snatching up the simple hat and shoes she'd left by the door, she fled.

Unlike her personal guards, who would have questioned her endlessly and insisted on escorting her into the city, the guards who were manning the towers outside the palace hardly stirred when she asked for the gate to be opened. Without guards and fine dresses, and with her bushel of hair tucked up and her face tucked down, she could pass for a servant in the shadows.

As soon as she was outside the gate, she started to run.

There were aristocrats milling around the tiled city streets, laughing and flirting in their fine clothes and glamours. Light spilled from open doorways, music danced along the window ledges, and everywhere was the smell of food and the clink of glasses and shadows kissing and sighing in darkened alleyways.

It was like this always in the city. The frivolity, the pleasure. The white city of Artemisia—their own little paradise beneath the protective glass.

At the center of it all was the dais, a circular platform where dramas were performed and auctions held, where spectacles of illusion and bawdy humor often drew the families from their mansions for a night of revelry.

Public humiliations and punishments were frequently on the docket.

Winter was panting, both frazzled and giddy with her success, as the dais came into view. She spotted him and the yearning inside her weakened her knees. She had to slow to catch her breath.

He was sitting with his back to the enormous sundial at the center of the dais, an instrument as useless as it was striking during these long nights. Ropes bound his bare arms and his chin was collapsed against his collarbone, pale hair hiding his face. As Winter neared him, she could see the raised hash marks of the lashings across his chest and abdomen, scattered with dried blood. There would be more on his back. His hand would be blistered from gripping the lash. *Self-inflicted*, Levana had proclaimed the punishment, but everyone knew Jacin would be under the control of a thaumaturge. There was nothing *self-inflicted* about it.

Aimery, she heard, had volunteered for the task. He had probably relished every wound.

Jacin raised his head as she reached the edge of the dais. Their eyes clashed, and she was staring at a man who had been beaten and bound and mocked and tormented all day and for a moment she was sure he was broken. Another one of the queen's broken toys.

But then one side of his mouth lifted, and the smile hit his startling blue eyes, and he was as bright and welcoming as the rising sun.

"Hey, Trouble," he said, leaning his head back against the dial.

With that, the terror from the past weeks slipped away. He was alive. He was home. He was still Jacin.

She pulled herself onto the dais. "Do you have any idea how

worried I've been?" she said, crossing to him. "I didn't know if you were dead or being held hostage, or if you'd been eaten by one of the queen's soldiers. It's been driving me mad not knowing."

He quirked an eyebrow at her.

She scowled. "Don't comment on that."

"I wouldn't dare." He rolled his shoulders as much as he could against his bindings. His wounds gapped and puckered with the movement and his face contorted in pain, but it was brief.

Pretending she hadn't noticed, Winter sat cross-legged in front of him, inspecting the wounds. Wanting to touch him. Terrified to touch him. That much, at least, had not changed. "Does it hurt very much?"

"Better than being at the bottom of the lake." His smile turned wry, lips chapped. "They'll move me to a suspension tank tomorrow night. Half a day and I'll be good as new." He squinted. "That's assuming you're not here to bring me food. I'd like to keep my tongue where it is, thank you."

"No food. Just a friendly face."

"Friendly." His gaze raked over her, his relaxed grin still in place. "That's an understatement."

She dipped her head, turning away to hide the three scars on her right cheek. For years, Winter had assumed that when people stared at her, it was because the scars disgusted them. A rare disfigurement in their world of perfection. But then a maid told her they weren't disgusted, they were in awe. She said the scars made Winter interesting to look at and somehow, odd as it was, even more beautiful. *Beautiful.* It was a word Winter had heard tossed around all her life. A beautiful child, a beautiful girl, a beautiful young lady, so beautiful, *too* beautiful . . . and the stares that attended the word never ceased to make her want to don a veil like her stepmother's and hide from the whispers.

Jacin was the one person who could make her feel beautiful without it seeming like a bad thing. She couldn't recall him ever using the word, or giving her any compliments, for that matter. They were always hidden behind careless jokes that made her heart pound.

"Don't tease," she said, flustered at the way he looked at her, at the way he always looked at her.

"Wasn't teasing," he said, all nonchalance.

In response, Winter reached out and punched him on the shoulder.

He flinched, and she gasped, remembering his wounds. But Jacin's chuckle was warm. "That's not a fair fight, Princess."

She reeled back the budding apology. "It's about time I had the advantage."

He glanced past her, into the streets. "Where's your guard?"

"I left him behind. Searching for a monster in my closet."

The sunshine smile hardened into exasperation. "Princess, you can't go out alone. If something happened to you—"

"Who's going to hurt me here, in the city? Everyone knows who I am."

"It just takes one idiot, too used to getting what he wants and too drunk to control himself."

She flushed and clenched her jaw.

Jacin frowned, immediately regretful. "Princess—"

"I'll run all the way back to the palace. I'll be fine."

He sighed, and she listed her head, wishing she'd brought some sort of medicinal salve for his cuts. Levana hadn't said anything about medicine, and the sight of him tied up and vulnerable—and shirtless, even if it was a bloodied shirtless— was making her fingers twitch in odd ways.

"I wanted to be alone with you," she said, focusing on his face. "We never get to be alone anymore."

"It's not proper for seventeen-year-old princesses to be alone with young men who have questionable intentions."

She laughed. "And what about young men who she's been best friends with since before she could walk?"

He shook his head. "Those are the worst."

She snorted—an actual snort of laughter that served to brighten Jacin's face again.

But the humor was bittersweet. The truth was, Jacin touched her only when he was helping her through a hallucination. Otherwise, he hadn't deliberately touched her in years. Not since she was fourteen and he was sixteen, and she'd tried to teach him the Eclipse Waltz with somewhat embarrassing results.

These days, she would have auctioned off the Milky Way to make his intentions a little less honorable.

Her smile started to fizzle. "I've missed you," she said.

His gaze dropped away and he shifted in an attempt to get more comfortable against the dial. Locking his jaw so she wouldn't see how much every tiny movement pained him. "How's your head?" he asked.

"The visions come and go," she said, "but they don't seem to be getting worse."

"Have you had one today?"

She picked at a small, natural flaw in the linen of her pants, thinking back. "No, not since the trials yesterday. I turned into a girl of icicles, and Aimery lost his head. Literally."

"Wouldn't mind if that last one came true."

She shushed him.

"I mean it. I don't like how he looks at you."

Winter glanced over her shoulder, but the courtyards surrounding the dais were empty. Only the distant bustle of music and laughter reminded her they were in a metropolis at all.

"You're back on Luna now," she said. "You have to be careful what you say."

"You're giving *me* advice on how to be covert?"

"Jacin—"

"There are three cameras on this square. Two on the lampposts behind you, one embedded in the oak tree behind the sundial. None of them have audio. Unless she's hiring lip-readers now?"

Winter glared. "How can you know for sure?"

"Surveillance was one of Sybil's specialties."

"Nevertheless, the queen could have killed you yesterday. You need to be careful."

"I know, Princess. I have no interest in returning to that throne room as anything other than a loyal guard."

A rumble overhead caught Winter's attention. Through the dome, the lights of a dozen spaceships were fading as they streaked across the star-scattered sky. Heading toward Earth.

"Soldiers," Jacin muttered. She couldn't tell if he meant it as a statement or a question. "How's the war effort?"

"No one tells me anything. But Her Majesty seems pleased with our victories . . . though still furious about the missing emperor, and the canceled wedding."

"Not canceled. Just delayed."

"Try telling her that."

He grunted.

Winter leaned forward on her elbows, cupping her chin. "Did the cyborg really have a device like you said? One that can keep people from being manipulated?"

A light sparked in his eyes, as if she'd reminded him of something important, but when he tried to lean toward her, his binds held him back. He grimaced and cursed beneath his breath.

Winter scooted closer to him, making up the distance herself.

"That's not all," he said. "Supposedly, this device can keep Lunars from using their gift in the first place."

"Yes, you mentioned that in the throne room."

His gaze burrowed into her. "*And* it will protect their minds. She said it keeps them from . . ."

Going crazy.

He didn't have to say it out loud, not when his face held so much hope, like he'd solved the world's greatest problem. His meaning hung between them.

Such a device could heal her.

Winter's fingers curled up and settled under her chin. "You said there weren't any more of them."

"No. But if we could find the patents for the invention . . . to even know it's possible . . ."

"The queen will do anything to keep more from being made."

His expression darkened. "I know, but I had to offer something. If only Sybil hadn't arrested me in the first place, ungrateful witch." Winter smiled, and when Jacin caught the look, his irritation melted away. "Doesn't matter. Now that I know it's possible, I'll find a way to do it."

"The visions are never so bad when you're around. They'll be better now that you're back."

His jaw tensed. "I'm sorry I left. I regretted it as soon as I realized what I'd done. It happened so fast, and then I couldn't come back for you. I'd just . . . abandoned you up here. With her. With *them.*"

"You didn't abandon me. You were taken hostage. You didn't have a choice."

He looked away.

She straightened. "You weren't manipulated?"

"Not the whole time," he whispered, like a confession. "I chose to side with them, when Sybil and I boarded their ship." Guilt washed over his face, and it was such an odd expression on him Winter wasn't sure she was interpreting it right. "Then I betrayed them." He thumped his head against the sundial, harder than necessary. "I'm such an idiot. You should hate me."

"You may be an idiot, but I assure you, you're quite a lovable one."

He shook his head. "You're the only person in the galaxy who would ever call me *lovable*."

"I'm the only person in the galaxy crazy enough to believe it. Now tell me what you've done that is worth hating you for."

He swallowed, hard. "That cyborg Her Majesty is searching for?"

"Linh Cinder."

"Yeah. Well, I thought she was just some crazy girl on a suicide mission, right? I figured she was going to get us all killed with these delusions of kidnapping the emperor and overthrowing the queen...to listen to her talk, anyone would have thought that. So I figured, I'd rather take a chance and come back to you, if I could. Let her throw her own life away."

"But Linh Cinder did kidnap the emperor. And she got away."

"I know." He shifted his attention back to Winter. "Sybil took one of her friends hostage, some girl named Scarlet. Don't suppose you know—"

Winter beamed. "Oh, yes. The queen gave her to me as a pet, and she's being kept in the menagerie. I like her a great deal."

Her brow creased. "Although I can't tell if she's decided to like me or not."

He flinched at a sudden unknown pain and spent a moment re-situating himself. "Can you get her a message for me?"

"Of course."

"You have to be careful. I won't tell you if you can't be discreet—for your own sake."

"I can be discreet."

Jacin looked skeptical.

"I *can*. I will be as secretive as a spy. As secretive as *you*." Winter scooted a bit closer.

His voice fell, as if he were no longer certain those cameras didn't come with audio. "Tell her they're coming for her."

Winter stared. "Coming for . . . coming here?"

He nodded, a subtle dip of his head. "And I think they might actually have a chance."

Frowning, Winter reached forward and tucked the strands of Jacin's sweat- and dirt-stained hair behind his ears. He tensed at the touch, but didn't pull away. "Jacin Clay, you're speaking in riddles."

"Linh Cinder." His voice became hardly more than a breath and she tilted closer yet to hear him. A curl of her hair fell against his shoulder. He licked his lips. "She's Selene."

Every muscle in her body tightened. She pulled back. "If Her Majesty heard you say—"

"I won't tell anyone else. But I had to tell you." His eyes crinkled at the corners, full of sympathy. "I know you loved her."

Her heart thumped. "My Selene?"

"Yes. But . . . I'm sorry, Princess. I don't think she remembers you."

Winter blinked, letting the daydream fill her up for one hazy moment. Selene, alive. Her cousin, her friend? *Alive.*

She scrunched her shoulders against her neck, casting the hope away. "No. She's dead. I was *there*, Jacin. I saw the aftermath of the fire."

"You didn't see *her.*"

"They found—"

"Charred flesh. I know."

"A pile of girl-shaped ashes."

"They were just ashes. Look, I didn't believe it either, but I do now." One corner of his mouth tilted up, into something like pride. "She's our lost princess. And she's coming home."

A throat cleared behind Winter and her skeleton nearly leaped from her skin. She swiveled her torso around, falling onto her elbow.

Her personal guard was standing beside the dais, scowling.

"Ah!" Heart fluttering with a thousand startled birds, Winter broke into a relieved smile. "Did you catch the monster?"

There was no return smile, not even a flush of his cheeks, which was the normal reaction when she let loose that particular look. Instead, his right eyebrow began to twitch.

"Your Highness. I have come to retrieve you and escort you back to the palace."

Righting herself, Winter clasped her hands in front of her chest. "Of course. It's so kind of you to worry after me." She glanced back at Jacin, who was eyeing the guard with distrust. No surprise. He eyed everyone with distrust. "I fear tomorrow will be even more difficult for you, Sir Clay. Do try to think of me when you can."

"*Try*, Princess?" He smirked up at her. "I can't seem to think of much else."

Four

CINDER LAY ON THE GROUND, STARING UP AT THE RAMPION'S vast engine, its ductwork, and revolving life-support module. The system blueprints she'd downloaded weeks ago were overlaid across her vision—a cyborg trick that had come in handy countless times when she was a working mechanic in New Beijing. She expanded the blueprint, zooming in on a cylinder the length of her arm. It was tucked near the engine room's wall. Coils of tubing sprouted from both sides.

"That has to be the problem," she muttered, dismissing the blueprint. She shimmied beneath the revolving module, dust bunnies gathering around her shoulders, and eased herself back to sitting. There was just enough space for her to squeeze in between the labyrinth of wires and coils, pipes and tubes.

Holding her breath, she pressed her ear against the cylinder. The metal was ice cold against her skin.

She waited. Listened. Adjusted the volume on her audio sensors.

What she heard was the door to the engine room opening.

Glancing back, she spotted the gray pants of a military

uniform in the yellowish light from the corridor. That could have been anyone on the ship, but the shiny black dress shoes . . .

"Hello?" said Kai.

Her heart thumped—every single time, her heart thumped.

"Back here."

Kai shut the door and crouched down on the far side of the room, framed between the jumble of thumping pistons and spinning fans. "What are you doing?"

"Checking the oxygen filters. One minute."

She placed her ear against the cylinder again. There—a faint clatter, like a pebble banging around inside. "*Aha.*"

She dug a wrench from her pocket and set to loosening the nuts on either side of the cylinder. As soon as it was free, the ship fell eerily quiet, like a humming that became noticeable only after it stopped. Kai's eyebrows shot upward.

Cinder peered into the cylinder's depths, before sticking her fingers in and pulling out a complicated filter. It was made of tiny channels and crevices, all lined with a thin gray film.

"No wonder the takeoffs have been rocky."

"I don't suppose you could use some help?"

"Nope. Unless you want to find me a broom."

"A broom?"

Raising the filter, Cinder banged the end of it on one of the overhead pipes. A dust cloud exploded around her, covering her hair and arms. Coughing, Cinder buried her nose in the crook of her elbow and kept banging until the biggest chunks had been dislodged.

"Ah. A broom. Right. There might be one up in the kitchen? . . . I mean, the galley."

Blinking the dust from her eyelashes, Cinder grinned at him. He was usually so self-assured that in the rare moments when he was flustered, it made all of her insides swap wrong side up. And he was flustered a lot lately. Since the moment he'd woken up aboard the Rampion, it was clear that Kai was twelve thousand kilometers outside of his element, yet he adapted well in the past weeks. He learned the terminology, he ate the canned and freeze-dried meals without complaint, he traded his fancy wedding clothes for the standard military uniform they all wore. He insisted on helping out where he could, even cooking a few of those bland meals, despite how Iko pointed out that—as he was their royal guest—*they* should be waiting on *him*. Thorne laughed, though, and the suggestion seemed to make Kai even more uncomfortable.

While Cinder couldn't imagine him abdicating his throne and setting off on a lifetime of space travel and adventure, it was rather adorable watching him try to fit in.

"I was kidding," she said. "Engine rooms are supposed to be dirty." She examined the filter again and, deeming it satisfactory, twisted it back into the cylinder and bolted it all in place. The humming started up again, but the pebble clatter was gone.

Cinder squirmed feetfirst out from beneath the module and ductwork. Still crouching, Kai peered down at her and smirked. "Iko's right. You really can't stay clean for more than five minutes."

"It's part of the job description." She sat up, sending a cascade of lint off her shoulders.

Kai brushed some of the larger chunks from her hair. "Where did you learn to do all this, anyway?"

"What, *that*? Anyone can clean an oxygen filter."

"Trust me, they can't." He settled his elbows on his knees and let his attention wander around the engine room. "You know what all this does?"

She followed the look—every wire, every manifold, every compression coil—and shrugged. "Pretty much. Except for that big, rotating thing in the corner. Can't figure it out. But how important could it be?"

Kai rolled his eyes.

Grasping a pipe, Cinder hauled herself to her feet and shoved the wrench back into her pocket. "I didn't learn it anywhere. I just look at things and figure out how they work. Once you know how something works, you can figure out how to fix it."

She tried to shake the last bits of dust from her hair, but there seemed to be an endless supply.

"Oh, you just *look* at something and figure out how it works," Kai deadpanned, standing beside her. "Is that all?"

Cinder fixed her ponytail and shrugged, suddenly embarrassed. "It's just mechanics."

Kai scooped an arm around her waist and pulled her against him. "No, it's impressive," he said, using the pad of his thumb to brush something off Cinder's cheek. "Not to mention, weirdly attractive," he said, before capturing her lips.

Cinder tensed briefly, before melting into the kiss. The rush was the same every time, coupled with surprise and a wave of giddiness. It was their seventeenth kiss (her brain interface was keeping a tally, somewhat against her will), and she wondered if she would ever get used to this feeling. Being *desired*, when she'd spent her life believing no one would ever see her as anything but a bizarre science experiment.

Especially not a boy.

Especially not *Kai*, who was smart and honorable and kind, and could have had any girl he wanted. *Any* girl.

She sighed against him, leaning into the embrace. Kai reached for an overhead pipe and pressed Cinder against the main computer console. She offered no resistance. Though her body wouldn't allow her to blush, there was an unfamiliar heat that flooded every inch of her when he was this close. Every nerve ending sparked and thrummed, and she knew he could kiss her another seventeen thousand times and she would never grow tired of it.

She tied her arms around his neck, molding their bodies together. The warmth of his chest seeped into her clothes. It felt nothing but right. Nothing but perfect.

But then there was the feeling, always lurking, always ready to cloud her contentment. The knowledge that this couldn't last.

Not so long as Kai was engaged to Levana.

Angry at the thought's invasion, she kissed Kai harder, but her thoughts continued to rebel. Even if they succeeded and Cinder was able to reclaim her throne, she would be expected to stay on Luna as their new queen. She was no expert, but it seemed problematic to carry on a relationship on two different planets—

Er, a planet and a moon.

Or whatever.

The point was, there would be 384,000 kilometers of space between her and Kai, which was a *lot* of space, and—

Kai smiled, breaking the kiss. "What's wrong?" he murmured against her mouth.

Cinder leaned back to look at him. His hair was getting longer, bordering on unkempt. As a prince, he'd always been groomed to near perfection. But then he became an emperor. The weeks since his coronation had been spent trying to stop a war, hunt down a wanted fugitive, avoid getting married, and endure his own kidnapping. As a result, haircuts became a dispensable luxury.

She hesitated before asking, "Do you ever think about the future?"

His expression turned wary. "Of course I do."

"And . . . does it include me?"

His gaze softened. Releasing the overhead pipe, he tucked a strand of hair behind her ear. "That depends on whether I'm thinking about the good future or the bad one."

Cinder tucked her head under his chin. "As long as one of them does."

"This is going to work," Kai said, speaking into her hair. "We're going to win."

She nodded, glad he couldn't see her face.

Defeating Levana and becoming Luna's queen was only the beginning of an entire galaxy's worth of worries. She so badly wanted to stay like this, cocooned in this spaceship, together and safe and alone . . . but that was the opposite of what was going to happen. Once they overthrew Levana, Kai would go back to being the emperor of the Eastern Commonwealth and, some-day, he was going to need an empress.

She might have a blood claim to Luna and the hope that the Lunar people would choose *anyone* over Levana, even a politically inept teenager who was made up of 36.28 percent cybernetic and manufactured materials. But she had seen the prejudices of the people in the Commonwealth. Something told her they wouldn't be as accepting of her as a ruler.

She wasn't even sure she wanted to be empress. She was still getting used to the idea of being a princess.

"One thing at a time," she whispered, trying to still her swirl-ing thoughts.

Kai kissed her temple (which her brain did not count as #18), then pulled away. "How's your training going?"

"Fine." She disentangled herself from his arms and glanced around the engine. "Oh, hey, while you're here, can you help me with this?" Cinder scooted around him and opened a panel on the wall, revealing a bundle of knotted wires.

"*That* was a subtle change of subject."

"I am not changing the subject," she said, although a forced clearing of her throat negated her denial. "I'm rewiring the orbital defaults so the ship's systems will run more efficiently while we're coasting. These cargo ships are made for frequent landings and takeoffs, not the constant—"

"Cinder."

She pursed her lips and unplugged a few wire connectors. "Training is going *fine*," she repeated. "Could you hand me the wire cutters on the floor?"

Kai scanned the ground, then grabbed two tools and held them up.

"Left hand," she said. He handed them to her. "Sparring with Wolf has gotten a lot easier. Although it's hard to tell if that's because I'm getting stronger, or because he's . . . you know."

She didn't have a word for it. Wolf had been a shadow of his former self since Scarlet had been captured. The only thing holding him together was his determination to get to Luna and rescue her as soon as possible.

"Either way," she added, "I think he's taught me as much about using my Lunar gift as he's going to be able to. From here on, I'll have to wing it." She examined the mess of wires, aligning it with a diagram over her retina display. "Not like that hasn't been my primary tactic this whole time." She furrowed her brow and made a few snips. "Here, hold these wires and don't let them touch."

Edging against her, Kai took hold of the wires she indicated. "What happens if they touch?"

"Oh, probably nothing, but there's a small chance the ship would self-destruct." Pulling out two of the fresh-cut wires, she began to twist them together into a new sequence.

Kai hardly breathed until she'd taken one of the threatening wires out of his grip. "Why don't you practice on me?" he said.

"Practice what?"

"You know. Your mind-manipulation thing."

She paused with the cutters hovering over a blue wire. "Absolutely not."

"Why?"

"I said I'd never manipulate you, and I'm sticking with that."

"It isn't manipulation if I know you're doing it." He hesitated. "At least, I don't think so. We could use a code word, so I'll know when you're controlling me. Like . . . what were those called again?"

"Wire cutters?"

"Like *wire cutters*."

"No."

"Or something else."

"I'm not practicing on you." Slipping the cutters into her pocket, she finished splicing the rest of the wires and relieved Kai of his duty. "There, we'll see how that goes."

"Cinder, I have nothing better to do. Literally, *nothing* better to do. My time on this ship has taught me that I have zero practical skills. I can't cook. I can't fix anything. I can't help Cress with surveillance. I know nothing about guns or fighting or . . . Mostly, I'm just a good talker, and that's only useful in politics."

"Let's not overlook your ability to make every girl swoon with just a smile."

It took Kai a moment to hear her over his frustration, but then his expression cleared and he grinned.

"Yep," she said, shutting the panel. "That's the one."

"I mean it, Cinder. I want to be useful. I want to help."

She turned back to face him. Frowned. Considered.

"*Wire cutters,*" she said.

He tensed, a trace of doubt clouding his expression. But then he lifted his chin. Trusting.

With the slightest nudge at Kai's will, she urged his arm to reach around her and pull the wrench from her back pocket. It was no more difficult than controlling her own cyborg limbs. A mere thought, and she could have him do anything.

Kai blinked at the tool. "That's wasn't so bad."

"Oh, Kai."

He glanced at her, then back to the wrench as his hand lifted the tool up to eye level and his fingers, no longer under his control, began to twirl the wrench—over one finger, under the other. Slow at first, then faster, until the gleaming of the metal looked like a magic trick.

Kai gaped, awestruck, but there was an edge of discomfort to it. "I always wondered how you did that."

"Kai."

He looked back at her, the wrench still dancing over his knuckles.

She shrugged. "It's too easy. I could do this while scaling a mountain, or . . . solving complex mathematical equations."

His eyes narrowed. "You have a *calculator* in your head."

Laughing, she released her hold on Kai's hand. Kai jumped back as the wrench clattered to the ground. Realizing he had control of his own limb again, he stooped to pick it up.

"That's beside the point," said Cinder. "With Wolf, there's some challenge, some focus required, but with Earthens . . ."

"All right, I get it. But what *can* I do? I feel so useless, milling around this ship while the war is going on, and you're all making plans, and I'm just waiting."

She grimaced at the frustration in his tone. Kai was responsible for billions of people, and she knew he felt like he had abandoned them, even if he hadn't been given a choice. Because *she* hadn't given him a choice.

He was kind to her. Since that first argument after he'd woken up aboard the Rampion, he was careful not to blame her for his frustrations. It was her fault, though. He knew it and she knew it and sometimes it felt like they were caught in a dance Cinder didn't know the steps to. Each of them avoiding this obvious truth so they didn't disrupt the mutual ground they'd discovered. The all-too-uncertain happiness they'd discovered.

"The only chance we have of succeeding," she said, "is if you can persuade Levana to host the wedding on Luna. So right now, you can be thinking about how you're going to accomplish that." Leaning forward, she pressed a soft kiss against his mouth. (*Eighteen.*) "Good thing you're such a great talker."

Five

SCARLET PRESSED HER BODY AGAINST THE STEEL BARS, straining to grasp the tree branch that dangled just outside her cage. Close—*so close.* The bar bit into her cheek. She flailed her fingers, brushing a leaf, a touch of bark—*yes!*

Her fingers closed around the branch. She dropped back into her cage, dragging the branch closer. Wriggling her other arm through the bars, she snapped off three leaf-covered twigs, then broke off the tip and let go. The branch swung upward and a cluster of tiny, unfamiliar nuts dropped onto her head.

Scarlet flinched and waited until the tree had stopped shaking before she turned the hood of her red sweatshirt inside out and shook out the nuts that had attacked her. They sort of looked like hazelnuts. If she could figure out a way to crack into them, they might not be a bad snack later.

A gentle scratching pulled her attention back to the situation. She peered across the menagerie's pathway, to the white wolf who was standing on his hind legs and batting at the bars of his own enclosure.

Scarlet had spent a lot of time wishing Ryu could leap over

those bars. His enclosure's wall was waist high and he should have been able to clear it easily. Then Scarlet could pet his fur, scratch his ears. What a luxury it would be to have a bit of contact. She had always been fond of the animals on the farm—at least until it was time to slaughter them and cook up a nice *ragoût*—but she never realized how much she appreciated their simple affection until she had been reduced to an animal herself.

Unfortunately, Ryu wouldn't be escaping his confinement any sooner than Scarlet would. According to Princess Winter, he had a chip embedded between his shoulder blades that would give him a painful shock if he tried to jump over the rail. The poor creature had learned to accept his habitat a long time ago.

Scarlet doubted she would ever accept hers.

"This is it," she said, grabbing her hard-earned treasure: three small twigs and a splintered branch. She held them up for the wolf to see. He yipped and did an enthusiastic dance along the enclosure wall. "I can't reach any more. You have to take your time with these."

Ryu's ears twitched.

Rising to her knees—as close to standing as she could get inside her cage—Scarlet grabbed hold of an overhead bar, took aim with one of the smaller twigs, and threw.

Ryu chased after it and snatched the stick from the air. Within seconds, he pranced back to his pile of sticks and dropped the twig on top. Pleased, he sat back on his haunches, tongue lolling.

"Good job, Ryu. Nice show of restraint." Sighing, Scarlet picked up another stick.

Ryu had just taken off when she heard the padding of feet down the path. Scarlet sat back on her heels, instantly tense, but relieved when she spotted a flowing cream-colored gown between the stalks of exotic flowers and drooping vines. The princess rounded the path's corner a moment later, basket in hand.

"Hello, friends," said Princess Winter.

Ryu dropped his newest stick onto the pile, then sat down, chest high as though he were showing her proper respect.

Scarlet scowled. "Suck-up."

Winter tilted her head in Scarlet's direction. A spiral of black hair fell across her cheek, obstructing her scars.

"What did you bring me today?" Scarlet asked. "Delusional mutterings with a side of crazy? Or is this one of your good days?"

The princess grinned and sat down in front of Scarlet's cage, uncaring that the path of tumbled black rock and ground covers would soil her dress. "This is one of my best days," she said, settling the basket on her lap, "for I have brought you a treat, with a side of news."

"Oh, oh, don't tell me. They're moving me to a bigger cage? Oh, please tell me this one comes with real plumbing. And maybe one of those fancy self-feeders the birds get?"

Though Scarlet's words were laced with sarcasm, in truth, a larger cage with real plumbing would have been a vast improvement. Without being able to stand up, her muscles were becoming weaker by the day, and it would be heaven if she didn't have to rely on the guards to lead her into the next enclosure, twice a day, where she was graciously escorted to a trough to do her business.

A *trough*.

Winter, immune as ever to the bite in Scarlet's tone, leaned forward with a secretive smile. "Jacin has returned."

Scarlet's brow twitched, her emotions at this statement pulling in a dozen directions. She knew Winter had a schoolgirl's crush on this Jacin guy, but Scarlet's one interaction with him had been when he was working for a thaumaturge, attacking her and her friends.

She'd convinced herself that he was dead, because the alternative was that he killed Wolf and Cinder, and that was unacceptable.

"And?" she prodded.

Winter's eyes sparkled. There were times when Scarlet felt like she'd hardened her heart to the girl's impeccable beauty—her thick hair and warm brown skin, her gold-tinged eyes and rosy lips. But then the princess would give her a look like *that* and Scarlet's heart would skip and she would once again wonder how it was possible this wasn't a glamour.

Winter's voice turned to a conspiratorial whisper. "Your friends are alive."

The simple statement sent the world spinning. Scarlet spent a moment in limbo, distrusting, unwilling to hope. "Are you sure?"

"I'm sure. He said that even the captain and the satellite girl were all right."

Like a marionette released, she drooped over her knees. "Oh, thank the stars."

They were *alive*. After nearly a month of subsisting on dogged stubbornness, finally Scarlet had a reason to hope. It was so sudden, so unexpected, she felt dizzy with euphoria.

"He also said to tell you," Winter continued, "that Wolf misses you very much. Well, Jacin's words were that he drove everyone rocket-mad with his pathetic whining about you. That's sweet, don't you think?"

Something cracked inside Scarlet. She hadn't cried once since she'd come to Luna—aside from tears of pain and delirium when she was tortured, mentally and physically. But now all the fear and all the panic and all the horror welled up inside her and she couldn't hold it back, couldn't even think beyond the onslaught of sobs and messy tears.

They were alive. They were all alive.

She knew Cinder was still out there—word had spread even to the menagerie that she had infiltrated New Beijing Palace and kidnapped the emperor. Scarlet had felt smug for days when the gossip reached her, even if she didn't have anything to do with the heist.

But no one mentioned accomplices. No one said anything about Wolf or Thorne or the satellite girl they'd been trying to rescue.

She swiped at her nose and pushed her greasy hair off her face. Winter was watching Scarlet's show of emotion like one might watch a butterfly shucking its cocoon.

"Thank you," said Scarlet, hiccuping back another sob. "Thank you for telling me."

"Of course. You're my friend."

Scarlet rubbed her palm across her eyes and, for the first time, didn't argue.

"And now for your treat."

"I'm not hungry." It was a lie, but she'd come to despise how much she relied on Winter's charity.

"But it's a sour apple petite. A Lunar delicacy that is—"

"One of your favorites, yeah, I know. But I'm not—"

"I think you should eat it." The princess's expression was innocent and meaningful all at once, in that peculiar way she had. "I think it will make you feel better," she continued, pushing a box through the bars. She waited until Scarlet had taken it from her, then stood and made her way across the path to Ryu. She crouched to give the wolf a loving scratch behind his ears, then leaned over the rail and started gathering up his pile of sticks.

Scarlet lifted the lid of the box, revealing the red marble-like candy in its bed of spun sugar. Winter had brought her many treats since her imprisonment, most of them laced with pain-killers. Though the pain from Scarlet's finger, which had been chopped off during her interrogation with the queen, had faded to a distant memory, the candies still helped with the aches and pains of life in such cramped quarters.

But as she lifted the candy from the box, she saw something unexpected tucked beneath it. A handwritten message.

Patience, friend. They're coming for you.

She closed the box fast before the security camera over her shoulder could see it, and shoved the candy into her mouth, heart thundering. She shut her eyes, hardly feeling the crack of the candy shell, hardly tasting the sweet-and-sour gooeyness inside.

"What you said at the trial," said Winter, returning with a bun-dle of sticks in her arms and laying them down where Scarlet could reach them. "I hadn't understood then, but I do now."

Scarlet swallowed too quickly. The candy went down hard, bits of shell scratching her throat. She coughed, wishing the princess had brought some water too. "Which part? I was under a lot of duress, you might recall."

"The part about Linh Cinder."

Ah. The part about Cinder being the lost Princess Selene. The true queen of Luna.

"What about it?" she said, bristling with suspicion. Had Jacin said something about Cinder's plans to reclaim her throne? And whose side was he on, if he spent weeks with her friends but had now returned to Levana?

Winter considered the question for a long time. "What is she like?"

Scarlet dug her tongue into her molars, thinking. What was Cinder like? She hadn't known her for all that long. She was a brilliant mechanic. She seemed to be honorable and brave and determined to do what needed to be done...but Scarlet suspected she wasn't always as confident as she tried to appear on the outside.

Also, she had a crush on Emperor Kai as big as Winter had on Jacin, although Cinder tried a lot harder to pretend otherwise.

But Scarlet didn't think that answered Winter's question. "She's not like Levana, if that's what you're wondering."

Winter exhaled, as if a fear had been released.

Ryu whined and rolled onto his back, missing their attention.

Winter grabbed a stick from the pile and tossed. The wolf scrambled back to his feet and raced after it.

"Your wolf friend," Winter said. "Is he one of the queen's?"

"Not anymore," Scarlet spat. Wolf would never belong to the queen again. Not if she could help it.

"But he *was*, and now he has betrayed her." The princess's tone had gone dreamy, her eyes staring off into space even after Ryu returned and dropped the stick beside his bars, beginning a new pile. "From what I know of her soldiers, that should not be possible. At least, not while they are under the control of their thaumaturge."

Suddenly warm, Scarlet unzipped her hoodie. It was filthy with dirt and sweat and blood, but wearing it still made her feel connected to Earth and the farm and her grandmother. It reminded her that she was human, despite being kept in a cage.

"Wolf's thaumaturge is dead," she said, "but Wolf fought against him even when he was alive."

"Perhaps they made a mistake with him, when they altered his nervous system."

"It wasn't a mistake." Scarlet smirked. "I know, they think they're so clever, giving soldiers the instincts of wild wolves. The instincts to hunt and kill. But look at Ryu." The wolf had lain down and was gnawing at the stick. "His instincts lean as much toward playing and loving. If he had a mate and cubs, then his instincts would be to protect them at all costs." Scarlet twirled the cord of her hoodie around a finger. "That's what Wolf did. He protected me."

She grabbed another stick from the pile outside her cage. Ryu's attention was piqued, but Scarlet only ran her fingers over the peeling bark. "I'm afraid I'll never see him again."

Winter reached through the bars and stroked Scarlet's hair with her knuckles. Scarlet tensed, but didn't pull away. Contact, any contact, was a gift.

"Do not worry," said Winter. "The queen will not kill you so long as you are my pet. You will have a chance to tell your Wolf that you love him."

Scarlet glowered. "I'm not your pet, just like Wolf isn't Levana's anymore." This time, she did pull back, and Winter let her hand fall into her lap. "And it's not that I *love* him. It's just ..."

She hesitated, and again Winter listed her head and peered at Scarlet with penetrating curiosity. It was unnerving, to think she was being psychoanalyzed by someone who frequently complained that the castle walls had started bleeding again.

"Wolf is all I have left," Scarlet clarified. She threw the stick halfheartedly across the path. It landed within paw's reach of

Ryu and he simply stared at it, like it wasn't worth the effort. Scarlet's shoulders slumped. "I need him as much as he needs me. But that doesn't make it love."

Winter lowered her lashes. "Actually, dear friend, 1 suspect that is *precisely* what makes it love."

Six

"THESE TWO NEWSFEEDS INCLUDE STATEMENTS FROM THAT waitress, Émilie Monfort," said Cress, trailing her fingers along the netscreen in the cargo bay, pulling up a picture of a blonde-haired girl speaking to a news crew. "She claims to be overseeing Benoit Farms and Gardens in Scarlet's absence. Here she makes a comment about the work getting to be a lot for her, and joked that if the Benoits don't return soon she might have to start auctioning off the chickens." Cress hesitated. "Or, maybe it wasn't a joke. I'm not sure. Oh, and here she talks about Thorne and Cinder coming to the farm and scaring her witless."

She glanced over her shoulder to see whether Wolf was still listening. His eyes were glued to the screen, his brow set, as silent and brooding as usual. When he said nothing, she cleared her throat and clicked to a new tab. "As far as the finances are concerned, Michelle Benoit did own the land outright, and these bank statements show that the property and business taxes continue to be automatically deducted. I'll set up payments to go through to the labor android rentals too. She missed last month's payment, but I'll make it up, and it looks like she's been a loyal customer long enough the missed payment didn't interrupt their work." She enlarged a grainy photo. "This satellite imagery is from thirty-six hours ago and shows the full team of androids and two human foremen working this crop." She shrugged and turned to face Wolf. "The bills are being paid, the animals are being tended, and the crops are being managed. Any accounts that were expecting regular deliveries are probably annoyed at Scarlet's absence, but that's the worst of it right now. I estimate it can go on being self-sustaining for . . . oh, another two to three months."

Wolf didn't take his forlorn stare from the satellite image. "She loves that farm."

"And it will be there waiting for her when we get her back." Cress sounded as optimistic as she could. She wanted to add that Scarlet was going to be fine, that every day they were getting closer to rescuing her—but she bit her tongue. The words had been tossed around so much lately they were beginning to lose their meaning, even to her.

The truth was that no one had any idea if Scarlet was still alive, or what shape they would find her in. Wolf knew that better than anyone.

"Is there anything else you want me to look up?"

He began to shake his head, but stopped. His eyes flashed to her, sharp with curiosity.

Cress gulped. Though she'd warmed to Wolf during her time aboard the ship, he still sort of terrified her.

"Can you find information about people on Luna?"

Her shoulders sank with an apology. "If I could have found out about her by now, I—"

"Not Scarlet," he said, his voice rough when he said her name. "I've been wondering about my parents."

She blinked. *Parents?* She had never imagined Wolf with parents. The idea of this hulking man having once been a dependent child didn't fit. In fact, she couldn't imagine any of the queen's soldiers having parents, having once been children, having once been loved. But of course they had—once.

"Oh. Right," she stammered, smoothing down the skirt of the worn cotton dress she'd taken from the satellite, what felt like ages ago. Though she'd spent a day wearing one of the military uniforms found in her crew quarters, a lifetime spent barefoot and in simple dresses had made the clothes feel heavy and cumbersome. Plus, all of the pants were way too long on her. "Do you think you might see them? When we're on Luna?"

"It's not a priority." He said it like a military general, but his expression carried more emotion than his voice. "But I wouldn't mind knowing if they're still alive. Maybe seeing them again, someday." His jaw flexed. "I was twelve when I was taken away. They must think *I'm* dead. Or a monster."

The statement resonated through her body, leaving her chest vibrating. For sixteen years, *her* father had thought she was dead too, while she'd been told that her parents had willingly sacrificed her to Luna's shell infanticide. She'd barely been reunited with her father before he died of letumosis, in the labs at New Beijing Palace. She'd tried to mourn his death, but mostly she mourned the idea of having a father at all and the loss of all the time they should have had to get to know each other.

She still thought of him as Dr. Erland, the odd, curmudgeonly old man who had started the cyborg draft in the Eastern Commonwealth. Who had dealt in shell trafficking in Africa.

He was also the man who helped Cinder escape from prison.

So many things he'd done—some good, some terrible. And

all, Cinder had told her, because he was determined to end Levana's rule.

To avenge his daughter. To avenge *her*.

"Cress?"

She jolted. "Sorry. 1 don't...1 can't access Luna's databases from here. But once we're on Luna—"

"Never mind. It doesn't matter." Wolf leaned against the cockpit wall and clawed his hands into his unkempt hair. He looked like he was on the verge of a meltdown, but that was his normal look these days. "Scarlet's the priority. The only priority."

Cress considered mentioning that overthrowing Levana and crowning Cinder as queen were decent-size priorities too, but she dared not.

"Have you mentioned your parents to Cinder?"

He cocked his head. "Why?"

"1 don't know. She mentioned not having any allies on Luna... how it would be useful to have more connections. Maybe they would help us?"

His gaze darkened, both thoughtful and annoyed. "It would put them in danger."

"1 think Cinder might intend to put a lot of people in danger." Cress worried at her lower lip, then sighed. "Is there anything else you need?"

"For time to move faster."

Cress wilted. "1 meant more like ... food, or something. When did you last eat?"

Wolf's shoulders hunched closer to his ears, and the guilty expression was all the answer she needed. She'd heard rumors of his insatiable appetite and the high-octane metabolism that kept him always fidgeting, always moving. She'd hardly seen any of that since coming aboard the ship, and she could tell that Cinder, in particular, was worried about him. Only when they were discussing strategies for Cinder's revolution did he seem rejuvenated—his fists flexing and tightening like the fighter he was meant to be.

"All right. I'm going to make you a sandwich." Standing, Cress gathered her courage, along with her most demanding voice, and planted a hand on her hip. "And *you* are going to eat it without argument. You need to keep up your strength if you're going to be of any use to us, and Scarlet."

Wolf raised an eyebrow at her newfound gumption.

Cress flushed. "Or . . . at least eat some canned fruit or something."

His expression softened. "A sandwich sounds good. With . . . tomatoes, if we have any left. Please."

"Of course." Drawing in a deep breath, she grabbed her portscreen and headed toward the galley.

"Cress?"

She paused and turned back, but Wolf was looking at the floor, his arms crossed. He looked about as awkward as she usually felt.

"Thank you."

Her heart expanded, ballooning with sympathy for him. Words of comfort sprang to her tongue—*She'll be all right. Scarlet will be all right*—but Cress stuffed them back down.

"You're welcome," she said, before turning into the corridor.

She had nearly reached the galley when she heard Thorne call her name. She paused and backtracked to the last door, left slightly ajar, and pressed it open. The captain's quarters were the largest of the crew cabins and the only room that didn't have bunks. Though Cress had been inside plenty of times to help him with the eyedrop solution Dr. Erland made in order to repair Thorne's damaged optical nerve, she never lingered long. Even with the door wide open, the room felt too intimate, too personal. There was a huge map of Earth on one wall, filled with Thorne's handwritten notes and markers indicating the places he'd been and the places he wanted to go, along with a dozen to-scale models of different spaceships scattered across the captain's desk, including a prominent one of a 214 Rampion. The bed was never made.

The first time she'd been in that room she asked Thorne about the map and listened, captivated, while he talked about the things he'd seen, from ancient ruins to thriving metropolises, tropical forests to white-sand beaches. His descriptions had filled Cress with longing. She was happy here on the spaceship—it was roomier than her satellite had been, and the bonds she was forming with the rest of the crew felt like friendship. But she had still seen so little of Earth, and the thought of seeing those things, while standing at Thorne's side, their fingers laced together . . . the fantasy made her pulse race every time.

Thorne was sitting in the middle of the floor, holding a portscreen at arm's length.

"Did you call me?" she asked.

A grin dawned on his face, impishly delighted. "Cress! I thought I heard your footsteps. Come here." He circled his whole arm, like he could draw her forward with the vacuum it created.

When she reached his side, Thorne flailed his hand around until he found her wrist and pulled her down beside him.

"It's finally working," he said, holding up the port again with his free hand.

Cress blinked at the small screen. A net drama was playing, though the feed was muted. "Was it broken?"

"No, the *solution.* It's working. I can see"—releasing her wrist, he waved a finger in the screen's direction—"kind of a bluish light. And the lights in the ceiling." He tilted his head back, eyes wide and pupils dilated as they tried to take in as much information as they could. "They're more yellow than the screen. That's it, though. Light and dark. Some blurry shadows."

"That's wonderful!" Although Dr. Erland believed Thorne's eyesight would begin to improve after a week or so, that week had come and gone with no change. It had now been nearly two weeks since the solution had run out, and she knew the wait had tried even Thorne's relentless optimism.

"I know." Crushing his eyes shut, Thorne lowered his head again. "Except, it's kind of giving me a headache."

"You shouldn't overdo it. You might strain them."

He nodded and pressed a hand over both eyes. "Maybe I should wear the blindfold again. Until things start to come into focus."

"It's up here." Cress stood and found the blindfold and the empty vial of eyedrops nestled among the model ships. When she turned around, Thorne was looking at her, or through her, his brow tense. She froze.

It had been a long time since he *looked* at her, and back then they'd been scrambling for their lives. That had been before he cut her hair too. She sometimes wondered how much he remembered about what she looked like, and what he would think when he saw her again . . . practically for the first time.

"I can see your shadow, sort of," he said, cocking his head. "Kind of a hazy silhouette."

Gulping, Cress folded the blindfold into his palm. "Give it

time," she said, pretending the thought of him inspecting her, seeing every unspoken confession written across her face, wasn't terrifying. "The doctor's notes said your optical nerve would continue to heal for weeks on its own."

"Let's hope it starts healing faster after this. I don't like seeing blurs and shadows." He twisted the blindfold between his fists. "One of these days, I just want to open my eyes and see you."

Heat rushed into her cheeks, but the depth of his words hadn't sunk in before Thorne laughed and scratched his ear. "I mean, and everyone else too, of course."

She smothered the start of a giddy smile, cursing herself for getting her hopes up again, for the thousandth time, when Thorne had made it quite clear he saw her as nothing more than a good friend, and a loyal member of his crew. He hadn't tried to kiss her again, not once since the battle atop the palace rooftop. And sometimes she thought he might be flirting with her, but then he'd start flirting with Cinder or Iko and she'd remember that a touch here or a smile there wasn't special to him like it was to her.

"Of course," she said, moving back toward the door. "Of course you want to see everyone."

She stifled a sigh, realizing she was going to have to train herself not to stare at him quite as often as she was used to, otherwise there would be no chance of hiding the fact that, despite all his attempts to persuade her otherwise, she was still hopelessly in love with him.

Seven

JACIN AWOKE WITH A JOLT. HE WAS DAMP AND STICKY AND smelled like sulfur. His throat and lungs were burning—not painfully, but like they'd been improperly treated and they wanted to make sure he knew about it. Instinct told him he was not in immediate danger, but the fuzziness of his thoughts set him on edge. When he peeled his eyes open, blaring overhead lights burst across his retinas. He grimaced, shutting them again.

Memories flooded in all at once. The trial. The lashings. The forty mind-numbing hours spent tied to that sundial. The mischievous smile Winter shared only with him. Being carted to the med-clinic and the doctor prepping his body for immersion.

He was still at the clinic, in the suspended-animation tank.

"Don't move," said a voice. "We're still disconnecting the umbilicals."

Umbilicals. The word sounded far too bloody and organic for this contraption they'd stuck him in.

There was a pinch in his arm and the tug of skin as a series of needles were pulled from his veins, then a snap of electrodes as sensors were pried off his chest and scalp, the cords tangling in his hair. He tested his eyes again, blinking into the brightness. A doctor's shadow hung over him.

"Can you sit?"

Jacin tested his fingers, curling them into the thick gel substance he was lying on. He grasped the sides of the tank and pulled himself up. He'd never been in one of these before—had never been injured enough to need it—and despite the confusion upon first waking, he already felt surprisingly lucid.

He looked down at his body, traces of the tank's blue gel-like substance still clinging to his belly button and the hairs on his legs and the towel they'd draped across his lap.

He touched one of the jagged scars that cut across his abdomen, looking as if it had healed years ago. Not bad.

The doctor handed him a child-size cup filled with syrupy orange liquid. Jacin eyed the doctor's crisp lab coat, the ID tag on his chest, the soft hands that were used to holding portscreens and syringes, not guns and knives. There was a pang of envy, a reminder that this was closer to the life he would have chosen, if he'd been given a choice. If Levana hadn't made the choice for him when she selected him for the royal guard. Though she'd never made the threat aloud, Jacin had known from the beginning that Winter would be punished if he ever stepped out of line.

His dream of being a doctor had stopped mattering a long time ago.

He shot back the drink, swallowing his thoughts along with it. Dreaming was for people with nothing better to do.

The medicine tasted bitter, but the burning in his throat began to fade.

When he handed the cup back to the doctor, he noticed a figure hovering near the doorway, ignored by the doctors and nurses who puttered around the storage cells of countless other tanks, checking diagnostics and making notations on their ports.

Thaumaturge Aimery Park. Looking smugger than ever in his fancy bright white coat. The queen's new favorite hound.

"Sir Jacin Clay. You look refreshed."

Jacin didn't know if his voice would work after being immersed in the tank, and he didn't want his first words to the thaumaturge to be a pathetic croak. He cleared his throat, though, and it felt almost normal.

"I am to retrieve you for an audience with Her Majesty. You may have forfeited your honored position in service to the royal entourage, but we still intend to find a use for you. I trust you are fit to return to active duty?"

Jacin tried not to look relieved. The last thing he wanted was to become the personal guard to the head thaumaturge again—especially now that Aimery was in the position. He embraced a particular loathing for this man, who was rumored to have abused more than one palace servant with his manipulations, and whose leering attentions landed far too often on Winter.

"I trust I am," he said. His voice was a little rusty, but not horrible. He swallowed again. "May I request a new uniform? A towel seems inappropriate for the position."

Aimery smirked. "A nurse will escort you to the showers, where a uniform will be waiting. I will meet you outside the armory when you're ready."

THE VAULTS BENEATH THE LUNAR PALACE WERE CARVED FROM years of emptied lava tubes, their walls made of rough black stone and lit by sparse glowing orbs. These underground places were never seen by the queen or her court, hence no one worried about making them beautiful to match the rest of the palace with its glossy white surfaces and crystalline, reflection-less windows.

Jacin sort of liked it down in the vaults. Down here, it was easy to forget he was beneath the capital at all. The white city of Artemisia, with its enormous crater lake and towering spires, had been built upon a solid foundation of brainwashing and manipulation. In comparison, the lava tubes were as cold and rough and natural as the landscape outside the domes. They were unpretentious. They did not do themselves up with lavish decorations and glitz in an attempt to conceal the horrible things that happened inside their walls.

Even still, Jacin moved briskly toward the armory. There was no residual pain, just the memory of each spiked lash and the betrayal of his own arm wielding the weapon. That betrayal was something he was used to, though. His body hadn't felt entirely his own since he became a member of the queen's guard.

At least he was home, for better or worse. Once again able to watch over his princess. Once again under Levana's thumb.

Fair trade.

He cleared Winter from his thoughts as he turned into the armory. She was a danger to his hard-earned neutrality. Thinking about her tended to give him an unwanted hitch in his lungs.

There was no sign of Aimery, but two guards stood at the barred door and a third sat at the desk inside, all wearing the gray-and-red uniforms of royal guards identical to Jacin's but for the metallic runes over the breast. Jacin ranked higher than any of them. He'd worried he would lose his position as a royal guard after his stint with Linh Cinder, but evidently his betrayal of her counted for something after all.

"Jacin Clay," he said, approaching the desk, "reporting for reinstatement under the order of Her Majesty."

The guard scanned a holograph chart and gave a terse nod. A second barred door filled up the wall behind him, hiding shelves of weaponry in its shadows. The man retrieved a bin that held a handgun and extra ammunition and pushed it across the desk, through the opening in the bars.

"There was also a knife."

The man scowled, as if a missing knife were the biggest hassle of his day, and crouched down to peer into the cupboard.

Jacin dropped the gun's magazine, reloading it while the man riffled through the cabinet. As Jacin was tucking the gun into his holster, the man tossed his knife onto the desk. It skidded across, off the surface. Jacin snatched it from the air just before the blade lodged itself in his thigh.

"Thanks," he muttered, turning.

"Traitor," one of the guards at the door said beneath his breath.

Jacin twirled the knife beneath the guard's nose and sank it into the scabbard on his belt without bothering to make eye contact. His early rise through the ranks had earned him plenty of enemies, morons who seemed to think Jacin had cheated somehow to earn such a desirable position so young. When really the queen just wanted to keep a closer eye on him and, through him, Winter.

The click of his boots echoed through the tunnel as he left them behind. He turned a corner and neither flinched nor slowed when he spotted Aimery waiting by the elevator.

When he was six steps away, Jacin came to a stop and clapped a fist to his chest.

Stepping aside, Aimery swooped his arm toward the elevator doors. The long white sleeve of his coat swung with it. "Let's not keep Her Majesty waiting."

Jacin entered without argument, taking up his usual spot beside the elevator's door, arms braced at his sides.

"Her Majesty and I have been discussing your role here since your trial," said Aimery once the doors had closed.

"I'm eager to be of service." Only years of practice disguised how abhorrent the words tasted in his mouth.

"As we wish to once again have faith in your loyalty."

"I will serve in whatever way Her Majesty sees fit."

"Good." There was that smile again, and this time it came with a suspicious chill. "Because Her Royal Highness, the princess herself, has made a request of you."

Jacin's gut tightened. There was no way to stay indifferent as his thoughts started to race.

Please, please, you hateful stars—don't let Winter have done something stupid.

"If your service meets with Her Majesty's expectations," Aimery continued, "we will return you to your previous position within the palace."

Jacin inclined his head. "I am most grateful for this opportunity to prove myself."

"I have no doubt of it, Sir Clay."

Eight

THE ELEVATOR DOORS OPENED INTO THE QUEEN'S SOLAR—AN
octagonal room made up of windows on all sides. The cylindri-
cal elevator itself was encapsulated in glass and stood at the
room's center so that no part of the view would be obstructed.
The décor was simple—thin white pillars and a glass dome overhead, mimicking the dome over the city. This tower, this very
room, was the highest point in Artemisia, and the sight of all
those buildings white and glittering beneath them, and an entire
jewelry case of stars overhead, was all the decoration the room
required.

Jacin had been there dozens of times with Sybil, but never for
his own audience with the queen. He forced himself to be unconcerned. If he was worried, the queen might detect it, and the
last thing he wanted was for anyone to question his loyalty to
the crown.

Though an elaborate chair was set on a raised platform, the
queen herself was standing at the windows. The glass was crystal clear and showed no hint of reflection. Jacin didn't know how

they'd managed to make glass like that, but the palace was full of it.

Sir Jerrico Solis, the captain of the guard and technically Jacin's superior, was also there, but Jacin didn't spare him a glance.

"My Queen," said Aimery, "you requested Sir Jacin Clay."

Jacin dropped to one knee as the queen turned. "You may stand, Jacin. How good of you to come."

Now, wasn't that sweet.

He did stand, daring to meet her gaze.

Queen Levana was horrifically beautiful, with coral-red lips and skin as pristine as white marble. It was all her glamour, of course. Everyone knew that, but it didn't make any difference. Looking at her could steal the breath of any mortal man.

However—and Jacin kept this thought very, very quiet in his head—the princess could steal both their breath *and* their heart.

"Sir Clay," said the queen, her voice a lullaby now compared with the harshness from the trial. "Aimery and I have been discussing your surprising yet joyful return. I would like to see you reinstated to your previous position soon. Our guard is weaker without you."

"I am yours to command."

"I've taken into consideration the comm you sent to Thaumaturge Mira prior to her death, along with two years of loyal service. I've also had a team looking into your claims about this ... *device* Linh Garan invented, and it seems you were correct. He unveiled a prototype he called a bioelectrical security device at an Earthen convention many years ago. As it happens, this discovery has also solved a mystery that my pack of special operatives in Paris had encountered earlier this year. We now know that Linh Cinder was not the only person to have had this device installed—but that her longtime protector, a woman named Michelle Benoit, had one too. We can only guess how many more might still exist."

Jacin said nothing, though his heart was expanding at this news. Cinder had seemed sure no more of these devices had been made, but maybe she was wrong. And if she was wrong . . . if there were more of them out there . . . he could get one for Winter. He could save her.

"No matter," said Levana, gliding a hand through the air. "We're already finding ways to ensure no such invention will ever come to the Earthen market. The reason I called you here was to discuss what is now to become of *you*. And I have a special role in mind, Sir Clay. One that I think you will not find disagreeable."

"My opinion means nothing."

"True, but the opinions of my stepdaughter do yet carry some weight. Princess Winter may not have been born with my blood, but I think the people acknowledge that she is a part of my family, a true darling among the court. And I did love her father so." She said this with a small sigh, though Jacin couldn't tell whether it was faked or not. She turned away.

"You know I was there when Evret was murdered," Levana continued, peering at the full Earth through the windows. "He died in my arms. His last plea was that I would take care of Winter, our sweet daughter. How old were you when he died, Jacin?"

He forced his shoulders to relax. "Eleven, Your Majesty."

"Do you remember him well?"

He clenched his teeth, not knowing what she wanted him to say. Winter's father and Jacin's father had both been royal guards and the closest of friends. Jacin had grown up with plenty of admiration for Evret Hayle, who had kept his position even after marrying Levana, then a princess. He stayed a guard even after Queen Channary died and Selene disappeared and Levana ascended to the throne. He often said he had no desire to sit on the throne beside her, and even less to sit around drinking wine and getting fat among the pompous families of Artemisia.

"I remember him well enough," he finally said.

"He was a good man."

"Yes, Your Majesty."

Her gaze slipped down to the fingers of her left hand. There was no wedding band there—at least, not that she was allowing him to see.

"I loved him very much," she repeated, and Jacin would have believed her if he believed she was capable of such a thing. "His death nearly killed me."

"Of course, My Queen."

Evret Hayle had been murdered by a power-hungry thaumaturge in the middle of the night, and Jacin still remembered how devastated Winter had been. How inadequate all of his attempts to comfort or distract her. He remembered listening to the sad gossip: how Evret had died protecting Levana, and how she had avenged him by plunging a knife into the thaumaturge's heart.

They said Levana had sobbed hysterically for hours.

"Yes, well." Levana sighed again. "As I held him dying, I promised to protect Winter—not that I wouldn't have regardless. She *is* my daughter, after all."

Jacin said nothing. His reserves of mindless agreements were running low.

"And what better way to protect her than to instate as her guard one whose concern for her well-being matches my own?" She smiled, but it had a hint of mocking to it. "In fact, Winter herself requested you be given the position as a member of her personal guard. Normally her suggestions are rooted in nonsense, but this time, even I have to acknowledge the idea has merit."

Jacin's heart thumped, despite his best efforts to remain disconnected. *Him?* On Winter's personal guard?

It was both a dream and a nightmare. The queen was right—no one else could be as trusted as he was to ensure her safety. In many ways, he'd considered himself Winter's personal guard already, with or without the title.

But being her guard was not the same as being her friend, and he already found it difficult enough to walk the line between the two.

"The changing of her guard happens at 19:00," said the queen, swaying back toward the windows. "You will report then."

He wet his throat. "Yes, My Queen." He turned to go.

"Oh, and Jacin?"

Dread slithered down his spine. Locking his jaw, he faced the queen again.

"You may not be aware that we have had . . . difficulties, in the past, with Winter's guard. She can be difficult to manage, given to childish games and fancies. She seems to have little respect for her role as a princess and a member of this court."

Jacin pressed his disgust down, down, into the pit of his stomach, where even he couldn't feel it. "What would you have me do?"

"I want you to keep her under control. My hope is that her affection for you will lend itself to some restraint on her part. I am sure you're aware that the girl is coming to be of a marriageable age. I have hopes for her, and I will not tolerate her bringing humiliation on this palace."

Marriageable age. Humiliation. Restraint. His disgust turned to a hard pebble, but his face was calm as he bowed. "Yes, My Queen."

WINTER STOOD WITH HER EAR PRESSED AGAINST THE DOOR of her private chambers, trying to slow her breathing to the point of dizziness. Anticipation crawled over her skin like a thousand tiny ants.

Silence in the hallway. Painful, agonizing silence.

Blowing a curl out of her face, she glanced at the holograph of Luna near her room's ceiling, showing the progression of sunlight and shadows and the standardized digital clock beneath it. 18:59.

She wiped her damp palms on her dress. Listened some more. Counted the seconds in her head.

There. Footsteps. The hard, steady thump of boots.

She bit her lip. Levana had given her no indication if Winter's request would be accepted—she didn't even know if her stepmother was going to *consider* the request—but it was possible. It was *possible.*

The guard who had been standing statuesque outside her chambers for the past four hours, relieved of duty, left. His footsteps were a perfect metronome to those that had just arrived.

There was a moment of shuffling as the new guard arranged himself against the corridor wall, the last line of defense should a spy or an assassin make an attack on the princess, and the first person responsible for whisking her away to safety should the security of Artemisia Palace ever be compromised.

She squeezed her eyes shut and fanned her fingers against the wall, as if she could feel his heartbeat through the stone.

Instead she felt something warm and sticky.

Gasping, she pulled away, finding her palm stained with blood.

Exasperated, she used the bloody hand to push her hair back, although it instantly tumbled forward again. "Not now," she hissed to whatever demon thought this was an appropriate time to give her visions.

She closed her eyes again and counted backward from ten. When she opened them, the blood was gone and her hand was clean.

With a whistled breath, Winter adjusted her gown and opened the door wide enough to poke her head out. She turned to the statue of a guard outside her door, and her heart swelled.

"Oh—she said yes!" she squealed, whipping the door open the rest of the way. She trotted around to face Jacin.

If he'd heard her, he didn't respond.

If he saw her, he showed no sign of it.

His expression was stone, his blue eyes focused on some point over her head.

Winter wilted, but it was from annoyance as much as disappointment. "Oh, please," she said, standing toe-to-toe, chest-to-chest, which was not simple. Jacin's flawless posture made her feel as if she were tilting backward, a breath away from falling over. "That's not necessary, is it?"

Five complete, agonizing seconds passed in which she could have been staring at a mannequin, before Jacin took in a slow breath and let it out all at once. His gaze dropped to hers.

That was all. Just the breath. Just the eyes.

But it made him human again, and she beamed. "I've been waiting all day to show you something. Come here."

Winter danced around him again, retreating back into her sitting parlor. She skipped to the desk on the other side of the room, where she'd draped her creation with a bedsheet. Taking hold of two corners, she turned back to the door.

And waited.

"Jacin?"

She waited some more.

Huffing, she released the sheet and stalked back toward the hall. Jacin hadn't moved. Winter crossed her arms over her chest and leaned against her door frame, inspecting him. Seeing Jacin in his guard uniform was always bittersweet. On one hand, it was impossible not to notice how very handsome and authoritative he looked in it. On the other hand, the uniform marked him as the property of the queen. Still, he was particularly striking today, all freshly healed from his trial and smelling of soap.

She knew that he knew that she was standing there, staring at him. It was infuriating how he could do such a blasted good job of ignoring her.

Tapping a finger against the flesh of her elbow, she deadpanned, "Sir Jacin Clay, there is an assassin under my bed."

His shoulders knotted. His jaw tensed. Three more seconds passed before he stepped away from the wall and marched into her chambers without looking her way. Past the covered surprise on the desk and straight through to her bedroom. Winter followed, shutting the door.

As soon as he reached the bed, Jacin knelt down and lifted the bed skirt.

"The assassin seems to have gotten away this time, Your Highness." Standing, he turned back to face her. "Do let me know if he returns."

He marched back toward the door, but she stepped in front of him and flashed a coquettish smile. "I certainly will," she said, bouncing on her toes. "But as long as you're here—"

"*Princess.*"

His tone was a warning, but she ignored him. Backing away

into the parlor, she tore the sheet away, revealing a table-size model of their solar system, the planets suspended from silk strings. "Ta-da!"

Jacin didn't come closer as she started fidgeting with the planets, but he also didn't leave.

Winter nudged the painted spheres into a slow orbit, each one moving separate from the others. "I had the idea when the engagement was first announced," she said, watching Earth complete a full circle around the sun before dragging to a stop. "It was going to be a wedding gift for Emperor Kaito, before ... well. Anyway, it's been a distraction while you were gone." Lashes fluttering, she risked a nervous glance up at Jacin. He was staring at the model. "It helps, you know, to focus on something. To think about the details."

It helped keep her thoughts in order, helped keep her sanity. She'd started having the hallucinations when she was thirteen, a little more than a year after she'd made the decision to never again use her glamour, to never again manipulate someone's thoughts or emotions, to never again fool herself into believing such an unnatural use of power could be harmless. Jacin, not yet a guard, had spent many hours with her, distracting her with games and projects and puzzles. Idleness had been her enemy for years. It was in those moments when her mind was most focused on a task, no matter how trivial, that she felt safest.

Making the model without him hadn't been as much fun, but she did enjoy the sensation of being in control of this tiny galaxy, when she was in control of so very little of her own life.

"What do you think?"

With a resigned sigh, Jacin stepped forward to examine the contraption that gave each planet its own orbital path. "How did you make it?"

"I commissioned Mr. Sanford in AR-5 to design and build the framework. But I did all the painting myself." She was pleased to see Jacin's impressed nod. "I hoped you might be able to help me with Saturn. It's the last one to be painted, and I thought—I'll take the rings, if you want to do the planet . . ." She trailed off. His expression had hardened again. Following his fingers, she saw him batting Luna around the Earth—the way Mr. Sanford had given Luna its own little orbit around the blue planet was nothing short of brilliant, in Winter's opinion.

"I'm sorry, Highness," said Jacin, standing upright again. "I'm on duty. I shouldn't even be in here, and you know that."

"I'm quite sure I *don't* know that. It seems you can guard me even better from in here than out there. What if someone comes in through the windows?"

His lips quirked into a wry smile. No one was going to come in through the windows, they both knew, but he didn't argue the point. Instead, he stepped closer and settled his hands on her shoulders. It was a rare, unexpected touch. Not quite the Eclipse Waltz, but her skin tingled all the same.

"I'm glad to be on your guard now," he said. "I would do anything for you. If you did have an assassin under your bed, I would take that bullet without a second thought, without anyone having to manipulate me."

She tried to interrupt him, but he talked over her.

"But when I'm on duty, that's all I can be. Your guard. Not your friend. Levana already knows I'm too close to you, that I care about you more than I should—"

Her brow drew together, and again she tried to interject, thinking *that* statement deserved further explanation, but he kept talking.

"—and I am not going to give her anything else to hold

over me. Or you. I'm not going to be another pawn in her game. Got it?"

Finally, a pause, and her head was swimming, trying to hold on to his declaration—*what do you* mean *you care about me more than you should?*—without contradicting his concerns.

"We are already pawns in her game," she said. "I have been a pawn in her game since the day she married my father, and you since the day you were conscripted into her guard."

His lips tensed and he moved to pull his hands away, the extended contact overstepping a thousand of his professional boundaries, but Winter reached up and wrapped her hands around his. She held them tight, bundling both of their hands between them.

"I just thought . . ." She hesitated, her attention caught on how much bigger his hands were compared with the last time she'd held them. It was a startling realization. "I thought it might be nice to step off the game board every now and then."

One of Jacin's thumbs rubbed against her fingers—just once, like a tic that had to be stifled.

"That would be nice," he said, "but it can't be while I'm on duty, and it really can't be behind closed doors."

Winter glanced past him, at the door she'd shut when he'd come in to check for a fictional assassin. "You're saying that I'm going to see you every day, but I have to go on pretending like I don't see you at all?"

He pried his hands away. "Something like that. I'm sorry, Princess." With a step back, he morphed seamlessly into the stoic guard. "I'll be in the corridor if you need me. *Really* need me."

After he'd gone, Winter stood gnawing at her lower lip, unable to ignore the momentary bits of elation that had slipped into the cracks of an otherwise disappointing meeting.

I care about you more than I should.

"Fine," she murmured to herself. "I can work with that."

She gathered up the little compact of paints, a few paint-brushes, and the fist-size model of Saturn waiting for its kaleido-scope of rings.

This time, Jacin started a little when she emerged in the corridor. The first time he'd been expecting her, but this must have been a surprise. She bit back a grin as she walked around to his other side and slid down the wall, planting herself on the floor next to him with crisscrossed legs. Humming to herself, she spread her painting supplies out before her.

"What are you doing?" Jacin muttered beneath his breath, though the hallway was empty.

Winter pretended to jump. "Oh, I'm so sorry," she said, peering up at him. "I'm afraid I didn't see you there."

He scowled.

Winking, she turned her attention back to her work, dipping a paintbrush into rich cerulean blue.

Jacin said nothing else. Neither did she. After the first ring was completed, she leaned her head against his thigh, making herself more comfortable as she picked out a sunburst orange. Over-head, Jacin sighed, and she felt the faintest brush of fingertips against her hair. A hint, a suggestion of togetherness, before he became a statue once more.

Nine

"EVAPORATED MILK ... KIDNEY BEANS ... TUNA ... MORE TUNA ... oh!" Cress nearly toppled headfirst into the crate as she reached for the bottom. She grabbed a jar and emerged victorious. "Pickled asparagus!"

Iko stopped digging through the crate beside her long enough to shoot her a glare. "You and your taste buds can stop bragging anytime now."

"Oh, sorry." Pressing her lips, Cress set the jar on the floor. "Good thing we opened this one. The galley was starting to look pretty scarce."

"More weapons in here," said Wolf, his shoulders knotted as he leaned over another one of the crates. "For a planet that's seen a century of world peace, you manufacture a lot of guns."

"There will always be criminals and violence," said Kai. "We still need law enforcement."

Wolf made a strangled sound, pulling everyone's attention toward him as he lifted a handgun from the crate. "It's just like the one Scarlet had." He flipped the gun in his palms, running his thumbs along the barrel. "She shot me in the arm once."

This confession was said with as much tenderness as if Scar-let had given him a bouquet of wildflowers rather than a bullet wound.

Cress and the others traded sorrowful looks.

Kai, who was standing nearest to Wolf, dropped a hand onto his shoulder. "If she's in Artemisia," he said, "I will find her. I promise."

A slight dip of his head was the only indication Wolf had heard him. Turning, he handed the gun, handle first, to Cinder, who was sitting cross-legged in the center of the cargo bay, organiz-ing what weaponry they had found. It was an impressive haul. It was a shame that when it came to fighting Lunars, weapons in the hands of their allies could be as dangerous as weapons in the hands of their enemies.

"This one's all medical supplies and common medicines," said Iko. "If we could find one with replacement escort-droid verte-brae and synthetic-tissue paneling, we'd be getting somewhere."

Cress smiled sympathetically. Iko was wearing the silk wrap top she'd worn to impersonate a member of the palace staff dur-ing the emperor's kidnapping, and its high collar almost covered the damage that had been done to her bionic neck and clavicle during the fight on the rooftop—but not quite. She'd gotten cre-ative with scraps of miscellaneous fabric to hide the rest of her injury, which was as much as they could do until Cinder had the parts to finish her repairs.

"Is this what I think it is?" Having returned his focus to his own crate, Kai held up a carved wooden doll adorned with be-draggled feathers and four too many eyes.

Cinder finished unloading the handgun and set it next to the others. "Don't tell me you've actually seen one of those hideous things before."

"Venezuelan dream dolls? We have some on display in the palace. They're incredibly rare." He examined its back. "What is it doing here?"

"I'm pretty sure Thorne stole it."

Kai's expression filled with clarity. "Ah. Of course." He nestled the doll back into its packaging. "He'd better plan on giving all this stuff back."

"Sure I'll give it back, Your Majesticness. For a proper finder's fee."

Cress swiveled around to see Thorne leaning against the cargo bay wall.

She blinked. Something was different about him. The blindfold he'd been wearing since his eyesight had begun to return weeks ago was now around his neck, and he was exceptionally clean-cut, like he'd gotten a closer shave than usual, and he was . . .

Electricity jolted down her spine.

He was *looking* at her.

No. Not just looking. There was an intense inspection behind that gaze, along with a curious bewilderment. He was surprised. Almost . . . *captivated.*

Heat rushed up her neck. She gulped, sure that she was imagining things.

Worldly, confident Captain Thorne could never be captivated by plain, awkward *her,* and she'd been disappointed by such wishful thinking before.

One corner of Thorne's mouth lifted. "The short hair," he said, with half a nod. "It works."

Cress reached up, grasping at the wispy ends that Iko had trimmed into something resembling a hairstyle.

"Oh!" said Iko, launching to her feet. "Captain! You can see!"

Thorne's attention skipped over to the android seconds before she launched herself over Cress and into his arms. Thorne stumbled against the wall and laughed.

"Iko?" Thorne said, holding her at arm's distance and drinking her in. The dark, flawless skin, the long legs, the braids dyed in varying shades of blue. Accepting the scrutiny, Iko gave a twirl. Thorne clicked his tongue. "Aces. I really know how to pick them, don't I?"

"Sight unseen," said Iko, flipping her braids off her shoulder.

Deflating, Cress began filling up her arms with canned goods. Definitely wishful thinking.

"Excellent," said Cinder, standing up and brushing off her hands. "I was beginning to worry we wouldn't have a pilot for when it's time to take Kai back to Earth. Now I just have to worry about not having a competent one."

Thorne leaned against the crate Cress was organizing. She froze, but when she dared to peer up through her lashes, his attention was on the other side of the cargo bay. "Oh, Cinder, I've missed seeing your face when you make sarcastic comments in an attempt to hide your true feelings about me."

"Please." Rolling her eyes, Cinder started organizing the guns against the wall.

"See that eye roll? It translates to 'How am I possibly keeping my hands off you, Captain?'"

"Yeah, keeping them from *strangling* you."

Kai folded his arms, grinning. "How come no one told me I had such steep competition?"

Cinder glared. "Don't encourage him."

With flushed cheeks, gritted teeth, and three stacks of cans cradled in her arms, Cress spun toward the main corridor—and sent the top can of peaches sailing off the stack.

Thorne snatched it from the air before Cress could gasp.

She froze, and for a moment it was there again—the way he was looking at her, causing the world to blur and her stomach to swoop. It was a good catch, to be sure, and she couldn't help but wonder if he'd been paying more attention to her than she thought.

Thorne beamed at the peaches. "Lightning-fast reflexes. Still got them." He took some canned corn off the stack. "Want help?"

She fixated on the cans. "No-thank-you-I've-got-it." Her words were all rushed and full of nerves as another blush flamed across her face. It occurred to her she'd been blushing from the moment he walked in, with his cavalier smile and his eyes that saw right through her.

She wanted to climb into one of those crates and pull down the lid. He hadn't had his eyesight back for five minutes and already she'd turned back into the anxious, giddy, flustered girl she'd been when they met.

"All right," Thorne said slowly, nestling the cans back into her arms. "If you insist."

Cress dodged around him and made her way to the galley. It was a relief to dump the food onto the counter and take a moment to stabilize herself.

So he could see again. It didn't change anything. He didn't think she was irresistible when he first saw her over that D-COMM link ages ago, and he wasn't going to think she was irresistible now. Especially not when Iko was right there. Android or not, she was the one with pearly teeth and coppery eyes and ...

Cress sighed, halting the envy before it could go any further. It wasn't Iko's fault Thorne wasn't interested in a tiny, skittish girl. In fact, she was happy for Iko, who took more delight in her new body than most humans ever did.

Cress just wished she could have half her confidence. If she had the guts to throw herself into Thorne's arms, to wink and make flirtatious comments and pretend like none of it mattered . . .

Except it *did* matter, or it would have, if she dared try it.

Just friends, she reminded herself. They were only friends, and would only be friends from here on out. It was a friendship that was to be cherished, as she cherished all the friendships she'd made aboard this ship. She wouldn't ruin it by wishing things could be more. She would be grateful for what affection she *did* have.

Cress let out a slow breath and stood straighter. It wouldn't be so hard, pretending this was all she wanted. Imagining she was satisfied with his companionship and platonic fondness. Now that he could see again, she would be extra vigilant in making sure any of her deeper feelings didn't show through.

Thorne was her friend and her captain, and nothing more.

When she returned to the cargo bay, the lightheartedness had dissipated. Hearing her, Thorne glanced over his shoulder, but she fixed her eyes resolutely on Kai.

"I understand this is sooner than we'd expected," Kai was saying, "but now that Thorne can finally see again, what are we waiting for? We can leave tomorrow. We could leave *now*."

Cinder shook her head. "There's so much to do. We still have the video to edit, and we haven't confirmed which route we're going to take to the outer sectors, and—"

"All things you don't need *my* help for," interrupted Kai. "All things you can be working on while I'm doing my part. People are dying every day. My people are being attacked at this very *moment*, and I can't do anything for them up here."

"I know. I know it's hard—"

"No, it's *torture.*" Kai lowered his voice. "But once you take me back, I can talk to Levana. Negotiate a new cease-fire and start putting our plan into motion—"

"Get to Scarlet sooner," said Wolf.

Cinder groaned. "Look, I get it. It's been a really long month and we're all anxious to move forward, it's just . . . our strategy—"

"Strategy? Look at us—we're spending our time unpacking *pickled asparagus.*" Kai shoved a hand through his hair. "How is this a good use of our time?"

"Every day we wait, our chances of success get better. Every day, more of her army is heading to Earth, leaving Levana and the capital unprotected. The weaker she is, the better chance we have of this revolution succeeding." She pointed at the netscreen, even though it was turned off. "Plus, the Union has been fighting back. She's lost a lot of soldiers already and maybe she's beginning to feel a little concerned?"

"She's not concerned," said Wolf.

Cinder frowned. "Well, at least she may have realized this war won't be won as easily as she'd hoped, which means she'll be that much more thrilled to hear Kai has returned and the wedding is back on. She'll be eager to reschedule it right away." She looped her fingers around her left wrist, where skin met metal.

Cress bit her lip, watching the fear and nerves flash across Cinder's face. Though she always did her best to hide it, Cress knew Cinder wasn't always as brave as she pretended. It was sort of comforting to think they might have this in common.

Kai's shoulders dropped and his voice lost its desperation when he took a step closer to her. "I understand you want to feel like you're ready—like we're all ready. But, Cinder . . . we're never going to feel that way. At some point, we have to stop planning and start doing. I think that time is now."

It took her a moment, but she finally met his gaze, then shifted to look at each of them in turn. Though Thorne was their captain, they all knew Cinder was the one that held them together.

"We're all risking our lives," she said. "I just don't want to risk them unnecessarily. I want to make sure we're prepared to—" She froze, her eyes unfocusing. Cress recognized the look from when Cinder was seeing something on her retina display.

Blinking rapidly, Cinder turned back to Kai, stunned. "Ship, turn on cargo bay netscreen, Commonwealth newsfeed."

Kai frowned. "What's going on?"

The netscreen flickered to life. It showed Kai's chief adviser—Konn Torin—standing at a podium. Before the audio signal could connect, though, Cinder said, "I'm so sorry, Kai. Your palace is under attack."

Ten

THEY WATCHED THE NEWSFEED IN SILENCE, THE CAMERAS trembling as android-manned hovers circled the palace below. Many of the gardens were smoking from fires set by the queen's soldiers, statues toppled and the massive gate torn to shreds, but the palace itself remained untouched. So far the single regiment of the Commonwealth's military stationed at the palace had kept the enemy at bay while they waited for reinforcements to arrive.

The siege on New Beijing Palace went against the strategies the wolf soldiers had been using throughout the war. They had become infamous for their guerilla attacks and scare tactics, as concerned with making the people of Earth terrified of them as they were with winning actual battles. To date, there had been no real *battles* at all—only skirmishes and surprise attacks, resulting in too much bloodshed and too many nightmares.

The wolf soldiers moved in packs, stealthy and quick. They caused havoc and destruction wherever they went, then disappeared before the Earthen military could catch up to them. There was speculation that they were moving through the sewers or disappearing into the wilderness, leaving a trail of blood and severed limbs in their wake. They were fond of leaving at least one witness alive in the aftermath to report on their brutality.

Again and again, their message was clear. *No one is safe.*

Earth had killed their share of the Lunar soldiers, as well as some of the thaumaturges that led each pack. They weren't invincible, as Earthen leaders pointed out again and again. But after 126 years of peace, the Earthen Union was unprepared to wage a war, especially one so unpredictable. For generations, their militaries had become more decorated social service workers than anything else, providing manual labor in impoverished communities and running supplies when natural disasters struck. Now, every country was scrambling to conscript more soldiers into their forces, to train them, to manufacture weaponry.

All the while, the Lunar soldiers decimated whole neighborhoods, leaving only the echo of their bloodthirsty howls behind.

Until now.

This attack on New Beijing Palace was the first time, as far as anyone could tell, multiple packs had come together in one orchestrated attack, and in broad daylight too. Cinder wondered if they were getting cocky, or if they were trying to make a statement. She tried to take solace in the fact that there were more wolf-mutant bodies lying on the palace grounds than she'd ever seen in one place—surely this battle would hurt their numbers, at least in New Beijing. But it was little comfort, when their blood was mixed with that of Earthen soldiers and one of the palace's towers was smoldering.

"The palace has been evacuated," said a journalist, speaking over the catastrophe in the video, "and all human officials and servants have been moved to safety. The secretary of defense commented in a speech only twenty minutes ago that they are not speculating at this time how long this siege might last, or how much destruction might be incurred. So far, military experts estimate upward of three hundred Commonwealth soldiers have been lost in this attack, and close to fifty Lunars."

"I feel so useless," Iko said, her tone deep with a misery only an android could understand. Iko was by no means a typical android, but she still managed to harbor one distinguishable trait all androids had been programmed with: the need to be useful.

On Cinder's other side was Kai, stricken. No doubt he was experiencing his own sense of uselessness. No doubt it was tearing him apart.

"The military will hold them," Cinder said.

He nodded, but his brow was drawn.

Sighing, she let her gaze travel from Kai to Wolf, Thorne to Cress to Iko. All watching the screen, determined and angry and horrified. Her attention swung back to Kai. He was veiling his emotions well, but she knew it was killing him. Watching his home burn. Having never had a home she cared about, at least not until she'd come aboard the Rampion, Cinder couldn't imagine the pain he was in.

She clenched her teeth, thinking of all their calculations, all their plans.

Kai was right. She would never feel ready, but they couldn't sit around doing nothing forever.

Thorne had his sight back.

Wolf had told her about his parents—laborers who had worked in factories and regolith mines all their lives. If they were alive, he thought they might be willing to offer them shelter on Luna. They might be allies.

The queen was making the boldest move she'd made since

the war started, which either meant she was getting overconfi-dent or she was getting desperate. Either way, Cinder didn't want Luna to win this battle. She didn't want them to have control of New Beijing Palace, even if it was merely symbolic. It was the home of the Commonwealth's royal family. It belonged to Kai, not Levana. *Never* Levana.

"We have had word," said the journalist, "that the radical po-litical group calling themselves the Association for Common-wealth Security has issued yet another statement calling for the forced abdication of Emperor Kaito, once again insisting that he cannot be the ruler we need in these troubled times, and that so long as he remains in the hands of terrorists, it is impossible for him to have the country's welfare as his primary concern. Though the ACS ideology has been largely ignored in main-stream politics, a recent net-based poll has indicated that their opinions are growing in popularity among the general public."

"Terrorists?" said Iko, looking around the group. "Does she mean *us*?"

Cinder dragged a frustrated hand down her face. Kai would be a great leader, *was* a great leader, but he hadn't yet been given the chance to prove himself. It made her stomach churn to think that his reign could be cut short, and all because of her.

She wanted to hug Kai and tell him they were idiots. They had no idea how much he cared about his country's welfare.

But that's not what he needed to hear.

Her retina display switched between her most-watched feeds. Body counts; death tolls; footage from the plague quaran-tines; teenagers standing in line outside recruitment centers, too many of them looking almost giddy to join the fight and de-fend their planet from this invasion. Levana in her sheer white veil.

She sent the feeds away.

Kai was watching her. "It's time, Cinder."

Time to say good-bye. Time to move ahead. Time to let go of the little utopia they'd cocooned themselves in.

"I know," she said, her voice sad and heavy. "Thorne, let's get ready to take Kai home."

Eleven

"THOUGHT I MIGHT FIND YOU DOWN HERE."

Cinder peeked around the side of the podship. Kai was loitering in the doorway, hands in his pockets, dressed again in his wedding finery.

She brushed some loose strands of hair off her forehead. "Just doing some basic maintenance," she said, disconnecting the power cell gauge from the podship and closing the hatch. "Making sure it's ready for your big return. I figured it was enough risk letting Thorne be your pilot; the least I could do is make sure the transport is in good condition."

"I wish you were coming with us."

"Yeah, me too, but we can't risk it."

"I know. It's just nice to have a mechanic on board. In case anything, you know . . . breaks." He scratched his ear.

"Oh, *that's* why you want me there. How flattering." Cinder wrapped the cord around the gauge and returned it to a cabinet bolted to the wall.

"That, and I'm going to miss you." His voice had gone soft, and it warmed the base of her stomach.

"With any luck, we'll see each other again soon."

"I know."

Cinder peeled off her work gloves and shoved them into her back pocket. There was still a tinge of panic at the action—her brain reminding her, out of habit, that she wasn't supposed to remove the gloves in front of anyone, especially Kai—but she ignored it. Kai didn't blink at the unveiling of her cyborg hand, like he didn't even notice it anymore.

She knew *she* was thinking about it less and less. Sometimes she was even surprised upon seeing a flash of metal in the corner of her eye when she went to pick something up. It was strange. She'd always been aware of it before, mortified that someone might see it.

"Are you scared?" she asked, pulling a wrench from her tool belt.

"Terrified," he said, but with a nonchalance that made her feel better about her own insides being wound into tight little knots. "But I'm ready to go back. I'm sure Torin is about to have a heart attack. And . . ." He shrugged. "I'm a little homesick."

"They'll be glad to have you back." Cinder knelt beside the ship, checking the bolts on the landing gear. She fit the wrench onto one, two, three bolts—none were loose. "Do you know what you're going to say to Levana?"

Kai crouched beside her, elbows braced against his knees. "I'm going to tell her I've fallen for one of my captors and the wedding is off."

Cinder's arm froze.

He smirked. "At least, that's what I wish I could tell her."

She blew a lock of hair out of her face and finished checking the bolts, before moving to the other side of the ship to repeat the process.

"I'm going to tell her I had nothing to do with the kidnapping," said Kai, donning what Cinder had come to think of as his *emperor voice*. "I'm in no way affiliated with you or the crew and I did my best to bargain for a quick release. I was a victim, held hostage, unable to escape. I'll probably make up something about inhumane treatment."

"Sounds about right."

"Then I'll *beg* her to marry me. Again." His lip curled with disgust.

Cinder couldn't blame him. The more she thought of it, the more she wanted to hijack this podship and head for Mars.

"When I see you again," said Kai, "I'll have clothes for everyone and new plating for Iko. If you think of anything else you need, Cress thinks she can get me an encrypted comm." He inhaled deeply. "Whatever happens, I'm on your side."

The sentiment both encouraged her and sent a shock of anxiety through her nerves. "I'm sorry to put you in so much danger."

"You're not," he said. "She was already going to kill me."

"You could try sounding a little more concerned when you say that."

"What is there to be concerned about?" His eyes glinted. "You're going to rescue me long before that happens."

Finished with the bolts, she stood and shoved the wrench back into her belt.

"Cinder . . ."

She froze, disconcerted at the serious edge in his voice.

"There's something I have to say before I go. In case—"

"Don't. Don't you even think this will be the last time we see each other."

A wistful smile touched his mouth, but quickly fled again. "I want to apologize."

"For suggesting this might be the last time we see each other? Because that *is* cruel, when here I am, trying to get some work done, and—"

"Cinder, listen to me."

She clenched her jaw shut and allowed Kai to take her shoulders, his thumbs tender against her collarbone. "I'm sorry about what happened at the ball. I'm sorry I didn't trust you. I'm sorry I . . . I said those things."

Cinder looked away. Though so much had changed between them since that night, it still felt like an ice pick in her heart when she remembered the way he'd looked at her, and his horrified words: *You're even more painful to look at than she is.*

"It doesn't matter anymore. You were in shock."

"I was an idiot. I'm ashamed at how I treated you. I should have had more faith in you."

"Please. You barely knew me. Then to find out all at once that I'm cyborg and Lunar . . . I wouldn't have trusted me either. Besides, you were under a lot of stress and—"

He tipped forward and kissed her on the forehead. The gentleness stilled her.

"You were still the girl who fixed Nainsi," he said. "You were still the girl who warned me about Levana's plans. You were still the girl who wanted to save her little sister."

She flinched at the mention of Peony, her younger stepsister. Her death was a wound that hadn't fully healed.

Kai's hands slipped down her arms, interlacing with her fingers—flesh and metal alike. "You were trying to protect yourself, and I should have tried harder to defend you."

Cinder gulped. "When you said I was even more painful to look at than Levana . . ."

Kai inhaled sharply, like the memory of the words hurt him as much as it hurt her.

"...do I...did I look like her? Does my glamour look like hers?"

A crease formed between his brows, and he stared at her, into her, before shaking his head. "Not exactly. You still looked like *you*, just..." He struggled for a word. "Perfect. A flawless version of you."

It was clear that it wasn't meant as a compliment.

"You mean, an unnatural version of me."

After a hesitation, he said, "I suppose so."

"I think it was instinct," she said. "I didn't realize I was using a glamour. I just knew I didn't want you to know I was a cyborg." A wry chuckle. "It seems so silly now."

"Good." He tugged her close again. "We must have made progress."

His lips had just brushed hers when the door opened.

"Got everything we need?" said Thorne, chipper as ever. Iko, Cress, and Wolf filed in after him.

Kai dropped Cinder's hands and she took a step back, adjusting her tool belt. "The pod's ready. Triple-checked. There shouldn't be any surprises."

"And the guest of honor?"

"I have everything I came with," said Kai, indicating his rumpled wedding clothes.

Iko stepped forward and handed Kai a box labeled PROTEIN OATS. "We have a gift for you too."

He flipped it over to the child's game printed on the back. "Yum?"

"*Open it*," said Iko, bouncing on her toes.

Prying open the top, Kai turned it over and dumped a thin

silver chain and a medallion into his palm. He lifted it up to eye level, inspecting the rather tarnished insignia. "'The American Republic 86th Space Regiment,'" he read. "I can see why it made you think of me."

"We found it in one of the old military uniforms," said Iko. "It's to remind you that you're one of us now, no matter what happens."

Kai grinned. "It's perfect." He looped the chain around his neck and tucked the medallion under his shirt. He gave Cress a quick farewell embrace, then pulled Iko into a hug. Iko squeaked, frozen.

When Kai pulled away, Iko looked from him, to Cinder, then back. Her eyes suddenly rolled up into her head and she collapsed onto the floor.

Kai jumped back. "What happened? Did I hit her power button or something?"

Frowning, Cinder took a step closer. "Iko, what are you doing?"

"Kai hugged me," said Iko, eyes still closed. "So I fainted."

With an awkward laugh, Kai turned to face Cinder. "You're not going to faint too, are you?"

"Doubtful."

Kai wrapped his arms around Cinder and kissed her, and though she wasn't used to having an audience, Cinder didn't hesitate to kiss him back. An impractical, uncalculating part of her brain told her to not let go. To not say good-bye.

The light mood was gone when they separated. He set his brow against hers, the tips of his hair brushing her cheeks. "I'm on your side," he said. "No matter what."

"I know."

Kai turned to face Wolf last. He lifted his chin and adjusted his fine shirt. "All right, I'm ready when you—"

The punch hit Kai square in the cheek, knocking him back into Cinder. Everyone gasped. Iko jerked upward with a surprised cry as Kai pressed a hand against his face.

"Sorry," said Wolf, cringing with guilt. "It's better when you don't see it coming."

"I somehow doubt that," said Kai, his words slurred.

Cinder pried his hand away to examine the wound, which was flaming red and already beginning to swell. "You didn't break the skin. He's fine. It'll bruise up nicely by the time he's back on Earth."

"Sorry," Wolf said again.

Kai gave his head a shake and didn't complain when Cinder pressed a kiss against his cheek. "Don't worry," she whispered. "It's weirdly attractive."

His laugh was wry, but appreciative. He kissed her one last time before hurrying into the podship, like he might change his mind if he stayed for another moment.

"Do I get a good-bye kiss too?" said Thorne, stepping in front of Cinder.

Scowling, Cinder shoved him away. "Wolf's not the only one who can throw a right hook around here."

Thorne chuckled and raised a suggestive eyebrow at Iko.

The android, still on the floor, shrugged apologetically. "I would love to give you a good-bye kiss, Captain, but that lingering embrace from His Majesty may have fried a few wires, and I'm afraid a kiss from you would melt my central processor."

"Oh, trust me," said Thorne, winking at her. "It would."

For an instant, while the joke was still written across his face, Thorne's gaze flickered hopefully toward Cress, but Cress was captivated by her own fingernails.

Then the look vanished and Thorne was marching to the pilot's side of the shuttle.

"Good luck," said Cinder, watching them adjust their harnesses.

Thorne gave her a quick salute, but it was Kai she was worried about. He tried to smile, still rubbing his cheekbone, as the doors sank down around them. "You too."

Twelve

KAI WATCHED THORNE'S HANDS, SEEMINGLY COMPETENT, AS they toggled a few switches on the podship's control panel. They emerged from the Rampion's dock and dove toward planet Earth. Thorne tapped some coordinates into the computer and Kai was surprised at the jolt of longing he felt to see the satellite imagery of the Commonwealth appear on the screen.

The plan was for Thorne to leave Kai at one of the royal safe houses—far enough from civilization that the podship should go undetected, if they were quick about it, but close enough to the city that Kai would be retrieved within an hour of alerting his security staff to his return.

"This must be weird for you," Thorne said, dragging his fingers across a radar screen. "Your cyborg girlfriend being a wanted outlaw and your fiancée's niece and all that."

Kai grimaced, which made his cheek start smarting again. "Honestly, I try not to think about the details." He shifted his gaze toward the Rampion as it receded fast from the viewing window. "Does she really call herself my girlfriend?"

"Oh, I wouldn't know. We haven't spent an evening gossiping and painting each other's toenails since the kidnapping."

Glaring, Kai leaned back against the headrest. "I'm already uncomfortable with you piloting this ship and being in control of my life. Try not to make it worse."

"Why does everyone think I'm such a bad pilot?"

"Cinder told me as much."

"Well, tell Cinder I'm perfectly capable of flying a blasted pod-ship without killing anyone. My flight instructor at Andromeda— which is a very prestigious military academy in the Republic, I will have you know—"

"I know what Andromeda Academy is."

"Yeah, well, my flight instructor said I was a natural."

"Right," Kai drawled. "Was that the same flight instructor who wrote in your official report about your inattentiveness, refusal to take safety precautions seriously, and overconfident attitude that often bordered on . . . what was the word she used? 'Fool-hardy,' I think?"

"Oh, yeah. Commander Reid. She had a thing for me." The radar blinked, picking up a cruiser in the far distance, and Thorne deftly changed directions to keep them out of its course. "I didn't realize I had a royal stalker. I'm flattered, Your Majesty."

"Even better—you had an entire government team assigned to digging up information on you. They reported twice daily for over a week. You did run off with the most-wanted criminal in the world, after all."

"And your girlfriend."

Kai smothered both a smile and a glare. "And my girlfriend," he conceded.

"It took them a week, huh? Cress could have laid out my whole biography within hours."

Kai pondered this. "Maybe I'll offer her a job when this is all over."

He expected it, and he wasn't disappointed—the irritated twitch beneath Thorne's eye. He hid it easily, though, his expression morphing into nonchalance. "Maybe you should."

Kai shook his head and looked away. Earth filled up the viewing window, a kaleidoscope of ocean and land. He gripped his harness, knowing they were hurtling through space at terrifying speeds, yet feeling like he was suspended in time for one still, quiet moment.

He let his shoulders settle, awed by the sight. The next time he would be up here—if all went according to plan—he'd be on his way to Luna.

"You know what's really strange to think about?" Kai said, as much to himself as to Thorne. "If Levana hadn't tried to kill Cinder when she was a kid, I might be engaged to *her* right now. She would already be queen. We could be plotting an alliance together."

"Yeah, but she would have been raised on Luna. And from what I can tell, being raised on Luna really messes people up. She wouldn't be the cuddly cyborg we've all come to adore."

"I know. I could have despised her as much as I despise Levana, though it's difficult to imagine."

Thorne nodded, and Kai was relieved he didn't say something obnoxious as the podship slipped into a bank of clouds. The light around them began to bend and brighten as they entered the first layers of Earth's atmosphere. The friction made the ship tremble and beads of water slicked back off the view window, but it wasn't long before they'd broken through. The Pacific Ocean sparkled beneath them.

"I suppose this is all pretty weird for you too," said Kai. "A wanted criminal, piloting a kidnapped political leader back to the country you first escaped from."

Thorne snorted. "The weird part is I'm not getting any ransom money out of it. Although, if you're feeling generous . . ."

"I'm not."

Thorne scowled.

"Well, maybe a little. You're set to serve time in three countries, right? The Commonwealth, America, and Australia?"

"Don't remind me. One would think the whole unionization thing would mean we could have a little consistency in our judicial systems, but, *no*, you commit crimes in three different countries and everyone wants to help dole out the punishment."

Kai pinched his lips, giving himself one last chance to reconsider. He'd only had the idea a few days ago, and his word would be gold once he said it aloud. He didn't want to set an unfair precedent as his country's leader, but at the same time—this felt *right*. And what was the point of being emperor if he couldn't sometimes do something just because it felt right?

"I might come to regret this," he said, dragging in a deep breath, "but, Carswell Thorne, I pardon all of your crimes against the Eastern Commonwealth."

Thorne whipped his focus toward Kai. The podship surged forward and Kai gasped, grabbing hold of his harness.

"Whoops, sorry." Thorne leveled the ship's nose and resumed their steady flight. "That was a, uh . . . an air . . . doldrum. Thing. But you were saying?"

Kai exhaled. "I'm saying you can consider your time served,

for the Commonwealth, at least. If we both survive this, when it's all over, I'll make it official. I can't do anything about the other countries, though, other than put in a good word for you. And to be honest, they'll probably think I'm crazy. Or suffering from Stockholm syndrome."

"Oh, you are *definitely* suffering from Stockholm syndrome, but I won't hold it against you. So—right. Great. Can I get this in writing?"

"No," said Kai, watching the podship controls as Thorne had his attention pinned on him again. "And the deal is only valid if we *both survive*."

"Mutual survival. Not a problem." Grinning, Thorne checked their course and made a few adjustments to his flight instruments as Japan appeared on the horizon.

"Also, I have one condition. You have to return everything you stole."

Thorne's grin started to fizzle, but he locked his hands around the console and brightened again. "Dream dolls and some surplus uniforms? Done."

"And?"

"And . . . and that's pretty much it. Aces, you make it sound like I'm a kleptomaniac or something."

Kai cleared his throat. "And the ship. You have to give back the ship."

Thorne's knuckles whitened. "But . . . she's my ship."

"No, she belongs to the American Republic. If you want a ship of your own, then you're going to have to work for it and buy one like everybody else."

"Hey, Mr. Born-into-Royalty, what do you know about it?" But Thorne's defensiveness faded as quickly as it had come, ending in a grumpy sulk. "Besides, I did work for it. Thievery isn't easy, you know."

"You're not really arguing with me about this, are you?"

Thorne clenched his eyes shut, and every muscle in Kai's body tensed, but then Thorne sighed and opened them again. "You don't get it. The Rampion and I have been through a lot together. I may have stolen her at first, but now it does feel like she belongs to me."

"But she *doesn't* belong to you. And you can't expect the rest of your crew to want to stay on in a stolen ship."

Thorne guffawed. "My crew? Let me tell you what's going to become of my crew when this is over." He ticked off on his fingers. "Cinder will be the ruling monarch of a big rock in the sky. Iko will go wherever Cinder goes, so let's assume she becomes the queen's hairdresser or something. You—are you a part of the crew now? Doesn't matter, we both know where you're going to end up. And once we get Scarlet back, she and Wolf are going to retire to some farm in France and have a litter of baby wolf cubs. *That's* what's going to become of my crew when this is done."

"It sounds like you've put some thought into this."

"Maybe," said Thorne, with a one-shoulder shrug. "They're the first crew I've ever had, and most of them even call me Captain. I'm going to miss them."

Kai squinted. "I notice you left out Cress. What's going on between you two, anyway?"

Thorne laughed. "What? Nothing's going on. We're . . . I mean, what do you mean?"

"I don't know. She seems more comfortable around you than anybody else on the ship. I just thought . . ."

"Oh, no, there's nothing like . . . we were in the desert together for a long time, but that's it." He ran his fingers absently over the podship controls but didn't touch anything. "She used to have a crush on me. Actually"—he chuckled again, but it was more strained this time—"she thought she was in love with me when we first met. Funny, right?"

Kai watched him from the corner of his eye. "Hilarious."

Thorne's knuckles whitened on the controls, then he glanced at Kai and started to shake his head. "What is this, a therapy session? It doesn't matter."

"It sort of matters. I like Cress." Kai shifted in the harness. "I like you too, despite my better judgment."

"You'd be surprised how often I hear that."

"Something tells me Cress might still like you too—against *her* better judgment."

Thorne sighed. "Yeah, that pretty much sums that up."

Kai cocked his head. "How so?"

"It's complicated."

"Oh, it's *complicated*. Because I have no idea what that's like." Kai snorted.

Thorne glared at him. "Whatever, Doctor. It's just, when Cress thought she was in love with me, she was actually in love with this other guy she'd made up in her head, who was all brave and selfless and stuff. I mean, he was a real catch, so who could blame her? Even I liked that guy. I kind of wish I *was* that guy." He shrugged.

"Are you so sure you're not?"

Thorne laughed.

Kai didn't.

"You're kidding, right?"

"Not really."

"Um, hi, I'm Carswell Thorne, a convicted criminal in your country. Have we met?"

Kai rolled his eyes. "I'm saying maybe you should stop putting so much energy into lamenting the fact that Cress was wrong about you, and start putting your energy into proving her right, instead."

"I appreciate the confidence, Your Imperial Psychologist, but we're way beyond that. Cress is over me and . . . it's for the best."

"But you do like her?"

When Thorne didn't respond, Kai glanced over to see Thorne's attention fixed on the cockpit window. Finally, Thorne responded, "Like I said, it doesn't matter."

Kai looked away. Somehow, Thorne's inability to talk about his attraction to Cress spoke so much louder than an outright confession. After all, he had no trouble making suggestive commentary about Cinder.

"Fine," he said. "So what *is* Cress going to do once this is all over?"

"I don't know," said Thorne. "Maybe she will go work for you on your royal stalking team."

Below, the blur of land became beaches and skyscrapers and Mount Fuji and, beyond it, an entire continent, lush and green and welcoming.

"I don't think that's what she would want, though," Thorne mused. "She wants to see the world after being trapped in that satellite her whole life. She wants to travel."

"Then I guess she should stay with you after all. What better way to travel than by spaceship?"

But Thorne shook his head, adamant. "No, believe me. She deserves a better life than this."

Kai leaned forward to better get a view of his home spreading out before them. "My point exactly."

Thirteen

"WHEN DID YOU LEARN TO *EMBROIDER?*" JACIN SAID, PICKING through the basket that hung on Winter's elbow.

She preened. "A few weeks ago."

Jacin lifted a hand towel from the collection and eyed the precise stitches that depicted a cluster of stars and planets around the towel's border. "Were you getting any sleep?"

"Not very much, no." She riffled through the basket and handed him a baby blanket embroidered with a school of fish swimming around the border. "This one's my favorite. It took four whole days."

He grunted. "I take it the visions were bad that week."

"Horrible," she said lightly. "But now I have all of these gifts." She took the blanket back from him and tucked it among the rest of the colorful fabrics. "You know keeping busy helps. It's when I'm idle the monsters come."

Jacin glanced at her from the corner of his eye. He had been her guard for weeks now, but rarely did they get to talk so casually or walk side by side like this—it was expected that guards keep a respectful distance from their charges. But today Winter had dragged him along to AR-2, one of the domes adjacent to the central sector. It was mostly high-end shops set among residential neighborhoods, but this early in the day all of the shops were still closed and the streets empty and peaceful. There was no one to care about propriety.

"And all these gifts are for the shopkeepers?"

"Shopkeepers, clerks, household servants." Her eyes glimmered. "The overlooked machine of Artemisia."

The lower classes, then. The people who dealt with the trash and cooked the food and ensured all the needs of Luna's aristocracy were met. They were rewarded with lives much more enviable than the laborers in the outer sectors. Full stomachs, at the least. The only downfall was that they had to live in Artemisia, surrounded by the politics and mind games of the city. A good servant was treated like a prized pet—spoiled and fawned over when they were wanted, beaten and discarded when they'd overstayed their usefulness.

Jacin had always thought that, given a choice, he'd rather take his luck to the mines or factories.

"You've been visiting them a lot?" he asked.

"Not as much as I'd like to. But one of the milliner's assistants had a baby and I've been meaning to make her something. Do you think she'll like it?"

"It'll be the nicest thing the kid has."

Winter gave a joyful skip as she walked. "My mother was a great seamstress, you know. She was becoming quite popular among the dress shops when—well. Anyway, she embroidered my baby blanket. Levana tried to throw it out, but Papa was able to stash it away. It's one of my most prized possessions." She fluttered her lashes and Jacin felt his lips twitch at her, rather against his will.

"I knew she was a seamstress," he said, "but how come I've never seen this special blanket of yours?"

"I was embarrassed to tell you about it."

He laughed, but when Winter didn't join him, the sound fizzled away. "Really?"

Winter shrugged, grinning her impish grin. "It's silly, isn't it? Holding on to a baby blanket, of all things?" She took in a deep breath. "But it's also my namesake. She embroidered a scene from Earth's winter, with snow and leafless trees and a pair of little red mittens. Those are like gloves, but with all the fingers joined together."

Jacin shook his head. "Embarrassed to show me. That's the stupidest thing I've ever heard."

"Fine. I'll show you, if you want to see it."

"Of course I want to see it." He was surprised how much her confession stung. He and Winter had shared everything since they were kids. It had never occurred to him she might harbor something like this, especially something so important as a gift from her mother, who had died in childbirth. But his mood brightened when he remembered—"Did I tell you I saw snow when I was on Earth?"

Winter stopped walking, her eyes going wide. "Real snow?"

"We had to hide the spaceship in Siberia, on this enormous tundra."

She was staring at him like she would tackle him if he didn't offer up more details.

Smirking, Jacin hooked his thumbs over his belt and rocked back on his heels. "That was all."

Winter smacked him in the chest. "That is not *all*. What was it like?"

He shrugged. "White. Blinding. And really cold."

"Did it glisten like diamonds?"

"Sometimes. When the sun hit it right."

"What did it smell like?"

He cringed. "I don't know, Win—Princess. Sort of like ice, I guess. I didn't spend much time outside. Mostly we were stuck on the ship."

Her gaze flickered with the almost slip of her name, something like disappointment that gave Jacin a shot of guilt.

So he smacked her back lightly on the shoulder. "Your parents did well. You're named after something beautiful. It's fitting."

"*Winter*," she whispered. Her expression turned speculative, the lights from a dress shop highlighting the specks of gray in her eyes.

Jacin tried not to be awkward when he looked away. There were times when she stood so close that he was amazed at his own ability to keep his hands to himself.

Moving the basket to her other arm, Winter started walking again. "Not everyone thinks I'm beautiful."

He scoffed. "Whoever told you that, they were lying. Or jealous. Probably both."

"*You* don't think I'm beautiful."

He snorted—somewhat uncontrollably—and laughed harder when she glared at him.

"That's funny?"

Schooling his expression, he mimicked her glare. "Keep saying things like that and people will start to think you've gone crazy."

She opened her mouth to refute. Hesitated. Nearly ran into a wall before Jacin scooped her back into the center of the narrow alley.

"You've never once called me beautiful," she said after his hand had fallen back to his side.

"In case you haven't noticed, you have an entire country of people singing your praises. Did you know they write poetry about you in the outer sectors? I had to listen to this drunk sing a whole ballad a few months back, all about your *goddess-like perfection*. I'm pretty sure the galaxy doesn't need my input on the matter."

She ducked her head, hiding her face behind a cascade of hair. Which was just as well. Jacin's cheeks had gone warm, which made him both self-conscious and irritated.

"*Your* input is the only input that matters," she whispered.

He stiffened, cutting a glance to her that she didn't return. It occurred to him that he may have led them into a topic he had no intentions of exploring further. Fantasies, sure. Wishes, all the time. But reality? No—this was taboo. This would end in nothing good.

She was a princess. Her stepmother was a tyrant who would marry Winter off to someone who was politically beneficial for her own desires.

Jacin was the opposite of politically beneficial.

But here they were, and there she was looking all pretty and rejected, and why had he opened his big, stupid mouth?

Jacin sighed, exasperated. With her. With himself. With this whole situation. "Come on, Princess. You know how I feel about you. *Everyone* knows how I feel about you."

Winter stopped again, but he kept walking, shaking his finger over his shoulder. "I'm not saying these things and looking at you at the same time, so keep up."

She scurried after him. "How do you feel about me?"

"No. That's it. That's all I'm saying. I am your *guard*. I am here to protect you and keep you out of trouble, and that's it. We are not swapping words that will result in a whole lot of awkward nights standing outside your bedroom door, got it?"

He was surprised at how angry he sounded—no, how angry he *felt*. Because it was impossible. It was impossible and unfair, and he had spent too many years in the trenches of unfairness to get riled up about it now.

Winter strode beside him, her fingers clenched around the basket handle. At least she wasn't trying to catch his eye anymore, which was a small mercy.

"I *do* know how you feel about me," she finally said, and it sounded like a confession. "I know that you are my guard, and you are my best friend. I know you would die for me. And I know that should that ever happen, I would die immediately after."

"Yeah," he said. "That's pretty much it." The sound of a nearby coffee grinder rumbled through the stone walkway, and the smell of baking bread assaulted his senses. He braced himself. "Also, I think you're sort of pretty. You know. On a good day."

She giggled and nudged him with her shoulder. He nudged her back and she stumbled into a flower planter, laughing harder now.

"You're sort of pretty too," she said. He threw a scowl at her, but it was impossible to hold on to when she was laughing like that.

"Your Highness!"

They both paused. Jacin stiffened, his hand going to his gun holster, but it was only a young girl watching them from the doorway of a little shop. A soap-filled bucket stood untouched at her feet and her eyes were as big as the full Earth.

"Oh, hello," said Winter, adjusting her basket. "Astrid, isn't it?"

The girl nodded, heat climbing up her cheeks as she gaped at the princess. "I—" She glanced toward the shop, then back to Winter. "Wait here!" she squealed, then dropped a rag into the bucket with a wet plop and rushed through the door.

Winter cocked her head to one side, her hair tumbling over her shoulder.

"You know that kid?"

"Her mother and father run this florist." She ran her fingers along a trailing vine in the window box.

Jacin grunted. "What does she want?"

"How should I know? I wish I'd brought them something . . ."

The girl reappeared, now with two younger boys in tow. "See? I told you she'd be back!" she was saying. The boys each paused to stare at Winter, their jaws hanging. The youngest was gripping a ring of twigs and dried flowers in both hands.

"Hello," said Winter, curtsying to each one. "I don't believe we've had the pleasure of meeting. I'm Winter."

When the boys couldn't find the courage to speak, Astrid answered, "These are my brothers, Your Highness, Dorsey and Dylan. I told them you bought flowers from our shop before and they didn't believe me."

"Well, it's true. I bought a posy of blue belldandies and kept them on my nightstand for a week."

"Wow," Dorsey breathed.

Winter smiled. "I'm sorry we can't stay to take a look through your shop this morning, but we're off to visit the milliner's assistant. Have you been to see the new baby yet?"

All three of them shook their heads. Then Astrid nudged the younger boy, Dylan, with her elbow. He jumped, but still couldn't bring himself to speak.

"We made something for you," said Astrid. "We've been waiting for you to come back. It's just . . . it's just from the leftovers, but . . ." She nudged her brother again, harder this time, and he finally held up the ring of flowers.

"What is this?" asked Winter, taking it into her hands.

Jacin frowned, then jolted as he realized what it was.

The older boy answered, "It's a crown, Your Highness. Took us almost a week of scrounging to get all the pieces." His cheeks were flushed bright red.

"I know it's not much," said the girl, "but it's for you."

The younger boy, having divested his gift, blurted suddenly, "You're *beautiful*," before ducking behind his brother.

Winter laughed. "You're all too kind. Thank you."

A hazy light caught Jacin's eye. Glancing upward, he spotted a nodule in the eaves of the next shop—a tiny camera watching over the shops and servants. There were thousands of identical cameras in sectors all over Luna, and he knew the chances of anyone minding the footage from a dull morning in AR-2 was unlikely, but a threatening chill still crept down his spine.

"The crown is lovely," Winter said, admiring the tiny white sprigs of flowers. She settled it on top of her thick black curls. "As splendid as the queen's jewels. I shall cherish it always."

With a growl, Jacin snatched the crown off her head and dropped it into the basket. "She will cherish it just as well in there," he snapped, his tone a warning. "The princess is busy. Go back inside, and don't go bragging about this to all your friends."

With frightened squeaks and wide eyes, the children couldn't have scurried back into the florist shop any faster. Grabbing Winter's elbow, Jacin dragged her away, though she soon ripped her arm out of his grip.

"Why did you do that?" she demanded.

"It looked bad."

"Accepting a gift from a few children? Honestly, Jacin, you don't have to be so mean."

"You could stand to be a little less *nice*," he spat back, scanning the walls and windows but not seeing any more cameras. "Putting it on your head. Are you insane?" She scowled at him and he scowled unapologetically back. "You're lucky no one saw." He gestured to the basket. "Cover it up before I rip it apart and bury it in one of these planters."

"You're overreacting," Winter said, though she did tuck a few of her hand towels around the mess of branches.

"You're not a queen, Princess."

Her gaze met his again, aghast. "I do not wish to be queen."

"Then stop accepting *crowns*."

Huffing, Winter turned away and marched on ahead—like a true princess would march ahead of her guard.

Fourteen

KAI WAITED UNTIL THORNE'S PODSHIP WAS A GLINT IN THE distance before he pulled out the portscreen Cinder had given him. Without an official ID chip confirming his identity, his comm to Royal Adviser Konn Torin was intercepted by the palace communications mainframe. The face of a young intern appeared.

"New Beijing Palace. How may I...direct..." Her eyes widened.

Kai smiled. "Emperor Kaito, for Royal Adviser Konn Torin, please."

"Y-yes, Your Majesty. Of course. Right away." Her cheeks bloomed red as she scrambled to redirect the commlink. Soon her image was replaced with Torin's.

"Your Majesty! Is it—are you—one moment. I'm stepping out of a meeting with the cabinet—are you all right?"

"I'm fine, Torin. But I'm ready to come home."

He heard the click of a door. "Where are you? Are you safe? Do you need—"

"I'll tell you everything when I get back. Right now I'm at our safe house on the Taihang terraces, and I'm alone. If you could alert the palace guard—"

"Right away, Your Majesty. We'll be there right away."

Torin suggested they keep the link open, afraid someone else would come for Kai before his own security team reached him. Although Cinder had ensured that the portscreen itself was untraceable, the link wasn't set up for direct communications and it was possible Lunars were listening in. But Kai knew Luna had lost their best method of surveillance when they'd lost Cress, so he insisted he was fine, he would be *fine*, before terminating the link.

He needed a moment to think before the whole galaxy spun out of control again.

Clipping the port to his belt, Kai climbed onto one of the large rocks overlooking the valley. He folded his legs beneath him, surprised at how calm he felt staring out at the terraces, plateaus that curled around the lush mountains, the teasing sparkle of a river winding at their feet. He could have gone inside the safe house to wait, but the weather was warm and there was a breeze that smelled like jasmine and it had been far too long since he'd admired the beautiful country he'd been born to.

After weeks aboard the Rampion, with its recycled air and reprocessed water, he was glad to be home.

And though he'd never seen Luna or its biodomes filled with artificial forests and man-made lakes, he was beginning to understand why Levana might want to dig her claws into Earth too.

Little time had passed when Kai heard the hum of engines. He kept his eye on the horizon, waiting for the podships. When they arrived, they arrived in force—a dozen military ships surrounding the safe house, many with guns drawn, and any number of personnel scanning the landscape for signs of a threat.

Squinting against the sunlight, Kai pushed his hair off his brow while the largest ship landed not far from the house. Uniformed officers poured out, establishing a perimeter and scanning for nearby life-forms, all jabbering into their headphones and holding ominous guns at the ready.

"Your Imperial Majesty," barked a gray-haired man, leading a team of four men up to him. "We are glad to see you, sir. Permission to conduct a security clearance scan?"

Kai pulled himself off the rock and handed the portscreen to one of the officers, who secured it in a crime evidence bag. He held out his arms while another officer dragged a scanner down his limbs.

"All clear. Welcome home, Your Majesty."

"Thank you. Where is Konn—"

A bang sent half a dozen personnel spinning toward the safe house, barking and leveling their guns at a cellar door that had burst open.

Konn Torin emerged, more harried than Kai had ever seen him. "Royal Adviser Konn Torin," he yelled, holding up his hands. His gaze flashed once over the guns, then landed on Kai near the edge of the plateau. His shoulders drooped with relief and as soon as one of the officers had scanned his wrist and confirmed his identity, Torin did something he had never done before.

He rushed toward Kai and hugged him.

The embrace was as quick as it was unexpected, before Torin pulled away and held Kai at arm's length, examining him. Kai was surprised to find he was slightly taller than Torin. That couldn't have happened in the past few weeks. Maybe he'd been taller for months and had never noticed. Having known Torin since he was a child, it was difficult to change his perception of him now.

Cinder told him that Torin had informed her of Kai's second

tracking chip. Maybe he was full of more surprises than Kai gave him credit for.

"Your face!" said Torin. "What did they do to you? She *promised* me—"

"I'm fine," said Kai, squeezing Torin's arm. "It's just a bruise. Don't worry about it."

"Don't worry—!"

"Your Majesty," interrupted the gray-haired man, "it may help to avoid media attention if you return through the safe house sublevels. We'll send a team to escort you."

Kai glanced around. A number of palace guards had emerged to join the flocking military. "If I'd known that was an option, I would have skipped this whole charade."

The officer didn't react.

"Yes, fine. Thank you for your thoroughness. Let's go."

Torin fell into step beside him, along with way too many guards, as they were ushered toward the cellar door.

"Nainsi will have tea waiting for you, and the chefs have been ordered to prepare refreshments for your return," said Torin. "The press secretary is drafting up a statement for the media, but you'll want to be briefed on the palace's official position regarding the security breach and kidnapping before we release anything."

Kai had to duck his head entering the house's basement. It was tidy, despite a few cobwebs in the corners, and as they headed into the passageways beneath the mountains they got brighter and cleaner.

"What's the status on the palace?" asked Kai.

"The enemy soldiers have not yet breached the palace walls. Our tactical analysts believe that if they do overrun the palace and discover there are no people to kill, they will redirect their attention to elsewhere. So far, we've found that these soldiers do not seem interested in general destruction or theft, only killing."

"Unless Levana is using the palace to make a statement. It would suggest they're winning."

"That is a possibility."

They rounded a corner and in the distance Kai could make out activity—talking and footsteps and the buzz of machinery. His entire staff was crammed into this labyrinth of rooms and hallways. He almost wished he'd stayed up on the terrace.

"Torin, what about the families of all these people? Are they safe?"

"Yes, sir. The families of all government officials were relocated to the palace within forty-eight hours of the first attacks. They are all here."

"And what about the people who aren't government officials? The chefs? The . . . the housekeepers?"

"I'm afraid we didn't have room for everyone. We would have brought down the whole city if we could."

Kai's gut clenched. He would have brought the whole *country* with him, if he could.

"Of course," he said, forcing himself not to dwell on the things he couldn't change. "Do I have an office down here? I need Nainsi to set up a meeting. This afternoon, if possible."

"Yes, Your Majesty. There are also private rooms set aside for the royal family. I'm having them made up now."

"Well, there's only one of me, and I only need one room. We can find something more useful to do with the rest of them."

"Of course. Who is Nainsi to contact for this meeting?"

He inhaled deeply. "My fiancée."

Torin's pace slowed and Kai thought he might come to a

complete stop, but Kai pulled his shoulders back and kept marching down the corridors. One of the guards ahead of them was yelling again—"Clear the way! Clear the way!"—as curious staff and officials emerged from doorways. Rumors were spreading fast and as Kai met the eyes of those he passed, he saw joy and relief cross their faces.

He gulped. It was strange to think how many people were worried about him—not just the people he saw every day, but citizens throughout the Commonwealth—waiting to hear if the kidnappers would return their emperor safely, having no idea that Linh Cinder was the last person in the world who would hurt him. It made him feel a little guilty for having enjoyed his time aboard the Rampion as much as he had.

"Your Majesty," said Torin, lowering his voice as he caught up with him again, "I must advise you to reconsider your arrangement with Queen Levana. We should at least discuss the best course of action before we make any hasty decisions."

Kai cut a glance toward his adviser. "Our government is being run out of an enormous bomb shelter and there are Lunar mutants beating down the doors of my palace. I'm not making hasty decisions. I'm doing what has to be done."

"What will the people think when they hear you intend to follow through with a marriage to the woman who is responsible for hundreds of thousands of deaths?"

"Millions. She's responsible for *millions* of deaths. But that doesn't change anything—we still need her letumosis antidote, and I'm hoping she'll accept the terms of a new cease-fire while we confirm alliance details."

One of the guards gestured toward an open door. "Your office, Your Majesty."

"Thank you. I require a moment of privacy with Konn-dàren, but if an android comes by with some tea, let her in."

"Yes, sir."

He stepped into the office. It was less lavish than his office in the palace, but not uncomfortable. Without windows, the room was filled with artificial light, but bamboo matting on the walls gave the space some warmth and helped deaden the sound of Kai's footsteps on the concrete floor. A large desk with a netscreen and half a dozen chairs took up the rest of the space.

Kai froze when his eyes landed on the desk and he started to laugh. On the corner of the desk sat a small, grime-filled cyborg foot. "You're kidding," he said, picking it up.

"I thought it was becoming a token of good luck," said Torin. "Although in hindsight, I can't imagine what led me to think that."

Smiling in amusement, Kai set Cinder's abandoned foot back down.

"Your Majesty," continued Torin, "what did you mean when you said Levana is already responsible for *millions* of deaths?"

Kai leaned against the desk. "We thought this war began when her special operatives attacked those first fifteen cities, but we were wrong. This war began when letumosis was manufactured in a Lunar laboratory and brought to Earth for the first time. All these years, she's been waging biological warfare on us, and we had no idea."

Though Torin was skilled at disguising his emotions, he couldn't hide his growing horror. "You're certain of this?"

"Yes. She wanted to weaken us, in population and resources, before she struck. I also suspect her ploy to offer an antidote as a bargaining chip was designed to create an immediate dependency on Luna—once she became empress."

"And you don't think this changes anything? Knowing it's all been a strategy to coerce you into this alliance, you still plan on going through with it? Your Majesty, there must be another way. Something we haven't considered yet." Torin's expression tightened. "I should inform you that in your absence, we've had a team focused on designing a new class of military-grade weaponry that will be able to penetrate even the biodomes on Luna."

Kai held his gaze. "We're building bombs."

"Yes. It's been a slow process. No Earthen military has built or harbored such weapons since the end of the Fourth World War, and there are unique modifications required to weaken Luna. But we believe that with Luna's limited resources and dependency on the domes to protect them—the success of a few bombs could mean a swift end to the war."

Kai stared down at his desk. All of Luna's population lived beneath specially designed biodomes that provided them with breathable atmosphere and artificial gravity and the ability to grow trees and crops. Destroying one of those protective barriers would kill everyone inside.

"How long before these weapons are ready?" he asked.

"We've finished the first prototype, and hope to have the first batch complete in four to six weeks. The fleet of spaceships required to transport the weapons is ready now."

Kai grimaced. He didn't want to say it, but he despised the thought of reducing Luna's cities to rubble. Already he had begun to think of Luna as belonging to Cinder, and he didn't want to destroy the kingdom that could someday be hers. But if it could end the war, and protect Earth . . .

"Keep me informed of any developments," he said, "and have the space fleet ready at a moment's notice. This is a last resort. First, we will try to reach a peaceful resolution. Unfortunately, that begins with appeasing Levana."

"Your Majesty, I beg you to reconsider. We are not *losing* this war. Not yet."

"But we aren't winning it, either." Kai's lips twitched upward. "And one thing has changed. Until now, Levana has been calling all the shots, but for the first time, I might be a step ahead of her."

Eyes narrowing, Torin took a step closer. "This isn't about an alliance at all, is it?"

"Oh, I fully intend to form an alliance with Luna." Kai glanced at the cyborg foot again. "I just intend to put a different queen on the throne first."

Fifteen

THE COMMUNICATION LINK TOOK AGES TO CONNECT, WHILE Kai stood before the netscreen with his hands clasped behind his back and his heart thudding louder than the Rampion's engine. He hadn't bothered to change from the white silk wedding shirt he'd been wearing when he'd been kidnapped, though it was wrinkled and had a tiny hole where Cinder's tranquilizer dart had punctured it. Still, he thought Levana might appreciate that contacting her was his first priority—above a fresh change of clothes, above even alerting the Earthen media to his return.

He was going to use every tactic he could think of to get on her good side. Anything to make this believable.

Finally, *finally*, the small globe in the corner stopped turning and the netscreen brightened, revealing Levana in her sheer white veil.

"Could it be my dear young emperor?" she cooed. "I had all but given you up for lost. What has it been, more than a month, I believe? I thought for sure your captors had murdered and dismembered you by now."

Kai smiled, pretending she'd made an amusing joke. "A few bumps and scratches here and there, but nothing so horrible as all that."

"I see," Levana mused, tilting her head. "That bruise on your cheek looks recent."

"More recent than some of the others, yes," said Kai. Pretending his time aboard the Rampion had been a trial, barely endured, was the first step in his strategy. "Linh Cinder made it clear from the start that I was a prisoner aboard her ship, not a guest. Between you and me, I think she was still bitter I'd had her arrested at the ball."

"How savage."

"I'm considering myself lucky for now. I was finally able to negotiate my freedom. I've just returned to New Beijing. Informing you of my return was my highest priority."

"And to what do we owe this happy occasion? I suspect those negotiations must have been cumbersome."

"My kidnappers had many demands. A monetary payout, of course, and also that I call off the ongoing search for the fugitives, both Linh Cinder and Carswell Thorne."

The veil fluttered as Levana adjusted her hands on her lap. "They must have believed their capture was imminent," she said, her tone unimpressed. "Although I can't see how that would be, given that you could not apprehend them whilst they were *in your own palace.*"

Kai's smile remained poised. "Nevertheless, I agreed to it. However, I made no guarantees for the rest of the Union, nor Luna. I expect these criminals will be found and brought to justice for their crimes, including my own assault and kidnapping."

"I expect they will," said Levana, and he knew she was

mocking him, but for the first time the knowledge didn't crawl beneath his skin.

"They had one additional demand." Behind his back, Kai squeezed his hands together, forcing his nervous energy into them. "They insisted that I refuse to follow through with the alliance terms you and I had agreed upon. They asked that the wedding not be allowed to continue."

"Ah," said the queen, with a spiteful laugh, "now we get to the reason that contacting me was such a high priority. I am sure it killed you to agree to such egregious terms."

"Not really," he deadpanned.

Levana leaned back, and he could see her shoulders trembling. "And why should these criminals concern themselves with intergalactic politics? Are they not aware that they are already responsible for starting a war between our nations? Do they not believe I will find a way to sit upon the Commonwealth throne regardless of your selfish bargain?"

Kai gulped painfully. "Perhaps their interest has to do with Linh Cinder's claim that she is the lost Princess Selene."

A silence crackled between him and the netscreen, still as ice on a pond.

"She seems to think," Kai continued, "that should we proceed with this wedding and coronation, it will weaken what claim she might have on the Lunar throne."

"I see." Levana had reclaimed her composure and her flippant, whimsical tone. "I had wondered if she would fill your head with falsehoods. I imagine you were a captive audience."

He shrugged. "It's a pretty small spaceship."

"You believe these claims of hers to be fact?"

"Honestly?" He steeled himself. "I don't care one way or the other. I have over five billion people living under my protection, and for the past month, every one of them has gone to bed wondering if this would be the night their home was attacked. If this was the night their windows would be broken, their children pulled from their beds, their neighbors mutilated in the streets, all by your ... by these *monsters* you've created. I can't—" He grimaced. This pain, at least, did not have to be faked. "I can't let this continue, and Linh Cinder, whether or not she is the lost princess, is not the one in charge of the Lunar military right now. I don't care about Lunar politics and family dynamics and conspiracy theories. I want this to end. And you're the one with the power to end it."

"A heartrending speech, young emperor. But our alliance is over."

"Is it? You seem convinced that I would bow to the whims of criminals and kidnappers."

She said nothing.

"You had my word long before I gave it to Linh Cinder. Therefore, I feel my agreement with you takes precedence. Wouldn't you agree?"

The veil shifted by her hands, like she was fidgeting with something. "I see that your time away has not diminished your impressive skills at diplomacy."

"I hope not."

"You're telling me that you wish to proceed with our previous arrangement?"

"Yes, under the same terms. We both agree to a cease-fire on all Earthen land and space territories, effective immediately. Upon your coronation as empress of the Eastern Commonwealth, all Lunar soldiers will be removed from Earthen soil, and you will allow us to manufacture and distribute your letumosis antidote."

"And what assurances can you give me that our wedding won't be subjected to the same mortifying spectacle as the last one? Surely your cyborg and her friends won't be pleased when they learn you've ignored their demands."

"I'm afraid I haven't had time to develop a plan. We'll increase security, of course. Bring in military reinforcements—I know how much you admire them."

Levana scoffed.

"But Linh Cinder has proven herself to be resourceful. One option would be to hold the ceremony in secret, and not release the proof of the wedding until after the coro—"

"No. I will not leave any question in the minds of the Earthen people that I am your wife, and their empress."

Kai's clenched his teeth to keep from gagging at the words. *Your wife. Their empress.* "I understand. We can consider other locations to host the ceremony, something more remote and secure. A spaceship, perhaps? Or even . . ."

He hesitated, trying to look appalled at his own unspoken thought.

"Or even what?"

"I was just . . . I doubt this would appeal to you. It would require a lot of work, and I don't know if it's even plausible . . . but, why not host the wedding on Luna? It would be impossible for Linh Cinder to interfere then."

Here, he paused, and tried not to seem like he was holding his breath.

The silence grew thick between them. Kai's heart began to pound.

It was too much. He'd made her suspicious.

Kai started to chuckle, shaking his head. "Never mind, it was a stupid idea." His mind whirred for another angle he could take.

"I'm sure we'll find a suitable location on Earth. I just need some time to—"

"You *are* clever, aren't you?"

His heart skipped. "Excuse me?"

The queen tittered. "Somewhere remote, somewhere secure. My darling emperor, of *course* we should host the wedding on Luna."

Kai paused, waited, then exhaled slowly, keeping his expression neutral. Another moment, and he remembered to even be skeptical. "Are you sure? We already have everything set up on Earth. All the transportation and accommodations, the catering, the announcements—"

"Don't be ridiculous." She fluttered her fingers behind the veil. "I don't know why I didn't think of it sooner. We will host the ceremony here in Artemisia. We have plenty of space for accommodations, and I have no doubt you will be pleased with the hospitality we can offer."

Kai pursed his lips, worried to dissuade her from the idea, and equally worried to appear too enthusiastic.

"Is this a problem, Your Imperial Majesty?"

"I don't doubt Artemisia is . . . lovely. But now that I'm considering it, I'm concerned this might alienate those guests who would have been privileged to attend the wedding here on Earth. In particular, the leaders of the Earthen Union."

"But of course the invitation will be extended to all Earthen diplomats. I would be disappointed if they didn't attend. After all, our union will be a symbol of peace, not only between Luna and the Commonwealth, but between Luna and all Earthen nations. I can extend the invitation to each of our Earthen guests personally, if you think that would be appropriate."

He scratched behind his ear. "With all due respect, there may be some . . . *hesitation* from the Union leaders. If I may be blunt, how can you guarantee that we—*they* won't be walking into a trap? You've made no attempts to disguise your threats against Earth and there are suspicions that you might still use your status as empress as a launchpad for, well . . ."

"World domination?"

"Precisely."

Levana tittered. "And what do you fear, exactly? That I might assassinate the heads of the Earthen Union while they're here, as a way of paving an easier path to taking control of their silly little countries?"

"*Precisely.*"

Another giddy laugh. "My dear emperor, this is an offer of peace. I want to earn the trust of the Union, not alienate them. You have my word that *all* Earthen guests will be treated with the utmost courtesy and respect."

Kai slowly, slowly let his shoulders relax. Not that he believed her for a minute, but it didn't matter. She had acted how he'd hoped she would.

"In fact," continued Levana, "as a show of my goodwill, I will agree to your request of an immediate cease-fire throughout the Union, and that cease-fire will be upheld in every Earthen territory whose leaders accept our invitation to attend the wedding here in Artemisia."

Kai flinched.

That was one way to increase attendance.

He rubbed his palms down the wrinkled fabric of his shirt. "I can't argue with the point that Artemisia is more secure than any place we could choose on Earth. I will discuss this with the leaders of the Earthen Union immediately."

"Please do, Your Majesty. As I'm sure the change of location will not be a problem, I'll begin making preparations for your visit, and our matrimonial and coronation ceremonies."

"Right, and . . . on that note. When would you like—"

"I suggest the eighth of November for our wedding and celebratory feast, followed by both coronations on the day following the new moon. We can schedule it to coincide with our sunrise—it is a beautiful time here on Luna."

Kai blinked. "That's . . . my days might be a little off, what with the whole hostage thing, but . . . isn't that only a week away?"

"Ten days, Your Majesty. This alliance has been deterred for too long. I do not believe anyone wishes to see my patience tried further. I do *so* look forward to receiving you and your guests." She dipped her head in a courteous farewell. "My ports will be ready to receive you."

Sixteen

THE AUDIO FEED DISCONNECTED WITH A SOFT CLICK, LEAVING the cargo bay in silence. Sitting atop one of the now-empty storage crates, Cress glanced around, taking in Cinder's tense shoulders as she stared at the blank netscreen, the way Wolf was tapping his fingers against his elbows, and Iko, who was still focused on the portscreen on her lap, trying to figure out her next move in the game she and Cress had been playing for the last hour.

"He did it," mumbled Cinder.

"Of course he did," said Iko, without looking up. "We knew he would."

Turning her back on the screen, Cinder scratched idly at her wrist. "The eighth is a lot sooner than I'd expected. I bet Earthen leaders will start departing within the next forty-eight hours."

"Good," said Wolf. "The wait is driving me crazy."

No, the separation from Scarlet was driving him crazy, Cress knew, but no one said anything. Maybe the wait was driving them all a little crazy.

"Jester to A1!" Iko finally announced. Beaming, she held the port out to Cress.

"King to C4, and I claim all rubies," said Cress, without hesitation.

Iko paused, looked down at the screen, and deflated. "How are you so good at this?"

Cress felt a rush of pride behind her sternum, although she wasn't sure if such a talent was impressive or embarrassing. "I played this a lot when I was bored on the satellite. And I got bored a lot."

"But my brain is supposed to be superior."

"I've only ever played against a computer if that makes you feel better."

"It doesn't." Iko crinkled her nose. "I want that diamond." Setting the port back into her lap, she fisted her hand around a ponytail of braids, once again deep in concentration.

Cinder cleared her throat, drawing Cress's focus, but not Iko's. "Kai will have a fleet with him. It's imperative we know which ship he's on."

Cress nodded. "I can find out."

"This plan will work," said Wolf forcefully, like he was threatening the plan itself. He started to pace between the cockpit and medbay. His and Cinder's anxiety made Cress more nervous than anything.

This was it, their only chance. Either it worked, or they failed.

"Crown-maker to A12."

It took Cress a moment to switch her thoughts back to the game. Iko had made the move she expected her to, the same move her computer aboard the satellite would have made.

Cress sacrificed her Jester, then proceeded to sneak her Thief across the board, snatching up every loose emerald, until even Iko's coveted diamond wouldn't win her the game.

"Ah! Why didn't I see that?" Growling, Iko pushed the portscreen away. "I never liked this game anyway."

"Podship detected," said the Rampion's monotone voice. Cress jumped, every muscle in her body tightening. "Captain Thorne is requesting permission to dock. Submitted code word: *Captain is King.*"

She exhaled, relieved not only that they hadn't been spotted by an enemy ship, but that Thorne was back. All the worry she'd been harboring since he and Kai had left rose to the surface of her skin and evaporated with a single breath.

"Permission granted," said Cinder, a fair amount of relief in her tone as well. She crossed her arms over her chest. "Step one complete. Kai is back on Earth, the wedding is rescheduled to take place on Luna, and Thorne has returned safely." She rocked back on her heels, a crease between her eyebrows. "I can't believe nothing went wrong."

"I would wait until you're sitting on a throne before making statements like that," said Wolf.

Cinder twisted her lips. "Good point. All right, everyone." She slapped her hands together. "Let's get started on any last-minute preparations. Cress and Iko, you're in charge of making final edits to the video. Wolf, I need you to—"

The door to the sublevel hatch burst open, crashing against the wall. Thorne heaved himself up the ladder and immediately rounded on Cinder, who took a startled step back.

"*You painted my ship?*" he yelled. "Why—what—why would you do that?"

Cinder opened her mouth, but hesitated. She had clearly expected a different sort of greeting. "Oh. That." She glanced around at Cress, Wolf, and Iko, like asking for backup. "I thought—wow, that was a long time ago. I guess I should have mentioned it."

"*Mentioned* it? You shouldn't have—! You can't go around painting someone else's ship! Do you know how long it took me to paint that girl in the first place?"

Cinder squinted one eye shut. "Judging from how precise and detailed it was, I'm going to guess . . . ten minutes? Fifteen?"

Thorne scowled.

"All right, I'm sorry. But the silhouette was too recognizable. It was a liability."

"A liability! *You're* a liability!" He pointed at Wolf. "He's a liability. Cress is a liability. We're *all* liabilities!"

"Am I one too?" asked Iko. "I don't want to be left out."

Thorne rolled his eyes and threw his hands into the air. "Whatever. It's *fine*. Not like it's *my* ship anyway, is it?" Growling, he dragged a hand through his hair. "I do wish you would have said something before I had a heart attack thinking I'd just hailed the wrong ship."

"You're right. Won't happen again." Cinder attempted a nervous smile. "So . . . how did it go?"

"Fine, fine." Thorne waved the question away. "Despite my inherent distrust of authority figures, I'm starting to like this emperor of yours."

Cinder raised an eyebrow. "I don't know if I should be relieved or worried."

Cress bit her cheek, burying an amused smile. She'd sensed some discomfort from Thorne when Kai had come aboard— after all, "Emperor" outranked "Captain" by just about anyone's standards—but she'd also noticed how Thorne stood a little straighter in Kai's presence, like he wanted the emperor to be impressed by him and his ship and his crew . . . just a little.

Shrugging off his jacket, Thorne draped it over the nearest crate. "Anything exciting happen while I was away?" For the first time, his gaze darted past Cinder and Iko to land on Cress, and the look was so sudden and focused she became instantly flustered. Tearing her gaze away, she set to inspecting the metal wall plating.

"The wedding is back on," said Cinder. "It will take place in Artemisia on the eighth, with the coronation to follow two days later at Lunar sunrise."

Thorne's eyebrows jumped upward. "Not wasting any time. Anything else?"

"Levana agreed to a cease-fire," said Wolf, "but we're waiting to hear if it's been implemented."

"Also, Cress destroyed me in a game of Mountain Miners," said Iko.

Thorne nodded, as if these two announcements carried the same weight. "She is a genius."

Cress's blush deepened, frustratingly. It had been easier to pretend she wasn't in love with him when he couldn't tell how often her gaze attached to him, how she blushed at every stray compliment.

"Yeah, but I'm an *android.*"

Thorne laughed, all anger over the painted ship gone. "Why don't you play Android Assault then? Maybe that'll give you an upper hand."

"Or Robot Resistance," suggested Cinder.

Thorne snapped his fingers. "*Yes.* Vintage quality." His eyes were twinkling, all calm and confident in that way that always made Cress feel more calm and confident too, just from being near him and knowing he was brave and capable and—

And he was looking at her. Again.

She looked away. Again.

Stupid, stupid, stupid.

Mortified, she found herself fantasizing about crawling down to the podship dock and getting sucked out into space.

"We should get started," Cinder said. "Pack what supplies we think we'll need, prepare the ship for extended neutral orbit."

"You mean abandonment," said Thorne, the lightness fading from his tone.

"I've already adjusted the wiring for the most efficient settings. It will be fine."

"You know that's not true. Without Cress disrupting the signals, it won't be long before the ship is found and confiscated."

Cinder sighed. "It's a risk we have to take. How about, once I'm queen, I'll use my royal coffers or whatever to buy you a new ship?"

Thorne glowered. "I don't want a new ship."

Cress felt a pang of sympathy. They were all sad to be leaving the Rampion. It had been a good home for the short time it sheltered them.

"You know, Thorne," said Cinder, speaking softly, like she didn't want to say what she was about to say, "you don't have to come with us. You could take us to Kai, then come back to the Rampion and . . . you know we would never give you away." She took in a deep breath. "I mean it. For all of you. You don't have to go with me. I know the danger I'm putting you in, and that you didn't know what you were signing up for when you joined me. You could go on with your lives, and I wouldn't stop you. Wolf, Cress, returning to Luna must feel like a death sentence to you both. And, Iko—"

Iko held up a hand. "You need a system debug if you're suggesting that I would abandon you now."

Thorne grinned. His self-assured, one-sided grin. "She's right. It's sweet of you to worry, but there's no way you can pull this off without us."

Pressing her lips, Cinder didn't argue.

Cress stayed silent, wondering if she was the only one who was briefly tempted by Cinder's offer. Returning to Luna *was* like sentencing themselves to death—especially a shell like her, who should have been killed years ago. Undermining Levana from the safety of space was one thing. But walking right into Artemisia . . . it was almost like asking to be killed.

But Thorne was right. Cinder needed them. All of them.

She shut her eyes and reminded herself to be brave.

"Besides," added Iko, breaking the tension, "our captain is still holding out for that reward money."

The others laughed and a smile fluttered over Cress's lips, but when she opened her eyes, Thorne wasn't laughing with the rest of them.

In fact, he looked suddenly uncomfortable, his shoulders tense. "Well, you know, some people might say that doing the right thing is a reward in itself."

The cargo bay fell still. Cress blinked.

Uncertainty stretched between them.

With a nervous chuckle, Thorne added, "But those people die poor and destitute, so who cares what they think?" He brushed away his own words. "Come on, freeloaders. Let's get to work."

Seventeen

KAI STARED OUT THE WINDOW, WATCHING THE CLOUDS
swirl over the continent below. He sought out the Great Wall
snaking across the Commonwealth and smiled to think his ancestors had built something even the Fourth World War couldn't
destroy.

He hoped this wouldn't be the last time he saw his beautiful
country.

He knew the danger he was putting himself in, along with
countless representatives from the rest of the Union. He hoped
Levana had been truthful when she said she meant them no
harm. He hoped this wasn't about to turn into a bloodbath in
which the naïve Earthens made for easy prey.

He hoped, but hoping did little to comfort him. He didn't
trust Levana. Not for a moment.

But this was the only way to give Cinder the chance she
needed to face Levana and start her rebellion. Cinder's success
would rid them all of Levana and her tyranny. No more plague.
No more war.

Stars, he hoped this worked.

Burying a sigh, he cast his restless gaze around the sitting room of his royal ship. If it weren't for the breathtaking view of Earth, Kai would have had no idea he was aboard a spaceship at all. The décor held all the old-world decadence of the palace: ornate lanterns and gilt wallpapers and a theme of flying bats carved into the crown moldings. Long ago, bats had been a symbol of good luck, but over the years they had come to symbolize safe travels through the darkness of space.

Torin caught his eye from an upholstered chair on the other side of the room, where he was busy reading his portscreen. He had insisted on coming to Luna, asserting that the Chair of National Security, Deshal Huy, would be capable of acting as head of the Commonwealth in their absence. Torin's place was beside Kai—for whatever it was worth.

"Is something wrong, Your Majesty?"

"Not so far." He rubbed his palms on his thighs. "You told the pilots I want to be informed if any ships hail us?"

"Of course. I wish I could tell you they found it to be a reasonable request, but they seemed understandably suspicious."

"Just as long as they do it."

"And you're sure this is a good idea?"

"Not in the slightest." The ship turned and Earth was no longer visible through the window. Kai turned away. "But I trust her."

Torin set down his port. "Then I have no choice but to trust her as well."

"Hey, you're the one who told her about my second tracking chip."

"Yes, and I have since wondered if that was the biggest mistake I've ever made."

"It wasn't." Kai rolled his shoulders, trying to relax. "Cinder can do this."

"You mean, Selene can do this."

"Selene. Cinder. She's the same person, Torin."

"I must disagree. To the world, Linh Cinder is a dangerous felon who kidnapped a world leader and instigated a war, while Princess Selene could be the solution to all our problems with Luna. By helping Linh Cinder, the world will think you're nothing but an infatuated teenager. By helping Selene, you're making a brave stand against our country's enemies and doing what you believe is best for the Commonwealth's future."

A wisp of a smile jotted across Kai's lips. "Whatever the world thinks, they *are* the same person. I want what's best for Cinder, and I want what's best for my country. Conveniently, I believe those are the same thing."

It had been a relief to tell Torin everything—the only person he trusted to keep his secrets. Cinder's identity, the real reason they were going to Luna, the revolution she planned to start there, and Kai's role in it all. Though Torin expressed concern that Kai was risking far too much, he hadn't tried to talk him out of it. In fact, Kai wondered if Torin wasn't developing a little bit of faith in Cinder as well, even if he tried to hide it behind cold cynicism.

Torin returned his attention to his portscreen, and Kai sat watching through the window, his heart skipping every time he spotted another ship against the backdrop of space.

Hours passed like days. Kai tried to take a nap, to no avail. He read over his wedding vows without comprehending a word. He paced back and forth, and drank half a cup of tea that some-one brought him—except it wasn't as good as Nainsi would have made, which made him miss his trusted android assistant. He'd come to rely on her practical, no-nonsense conversation, but Levana was adamant that no androids would be allowed on Luna, so he was forced to leave Nainsi behind.

He set the tea aside, his stomach writhing with nerves. He should have heard from Cinder by now. Something had gone wrong, and here he was flying an entire fleet of Earth's most powerful people right into Levana's clutches and it would all be for nothing and—

"Your Majesty?"

His head snapped up. The ship's first mate stood in the doorway.

"Yes?"

"We've been hailed by the American Republic's secretary of defense. It seems they're having technical issues with their ship's computer mainframe and have requested permission to board and complete the trip to Artemisia with us."

Kai exhaled.

"The captain suggests we send one of the military escorts to assist them. I'm happy to put them in touch—"

"That won't be necessary," said Kai. "We have the room. Let them board." Though a dozen province representatives and some journalists from the Commonwealth media were already aboard, the ship was nowhere near capacity.

The officer frowned. "I do believe it's a matter of security, not space. Due to their technical difficulties, we've been unable to obtain a proper ID on the ship or its officers. Their vid-comm is also malfunctioning. Our visual of the ship does confirm it as a Republic military ship, Rampion class, but beyond that we're forced to take them at their word, and I'm sure I don't need to remind Your Majesty that . . . your kidnappers were also in a Rampion."

Kai pretended to consider his point. "The Rampion I was held hostage aboard had the silhouette of a lady painted on its port side. Is there such a marking on the secretary's ship?"

The officer relayed the question into a comm-chip on his collar, and a moment later confirmed that no such lady was visible. Only black paneling on the boarding ramp.

"There you have it," said Kai, attempting nonchalance. "We will accept our American allies on board, assuming their pod-ships are in working order. In fact, why don't I come down to the dock to greet them, as a show of political goodwill?"

"I'll come as well," said Torin, setting his port aside.

The first mate looked like he wanted to object but, after an uncertain moment, clicked his heels together and nodded. "Of course, Your Majesty."

EVEN THE WAITING ROOM OUTSIDE THE PODSHIP DOCK WAS luxurious and Kai found himself tapping his foot on thick carpet while machinery hummed in the surrounding walls. The ship's captain had joined them, waiting to greet their guests before returning to the bridge, and he and the first mate stood with impeccable posture in their unwrinkled uniforms.

The screen beside the sealed doors announced that the dock was safe to enter.

The captain went first, Kai right behind him. There were six of their own podships waiting, and empty spaces for three more. The Rampion's shuttle had taken the farthest spot and sat with its engines powering down.

The two doors rose simultaneously and five people emerged—America's secretary of defense, one assistant, one intern, and two security agents.

The captain shook the secretary's hand, welcoming the new-comers aboard, followed by a series of diplomatic bows.

"Thank you for your hospitality. We do apologize for any inconvenience this may have caused," said the secretary, as Kai tried to figure out who this was beneath the illusion. He guessed Thorne and Wolf were the security agents, but the glamour being cast for the Republic's secretary was perfect, straight down to the mole on the right side of her chin. The assistant and intern were equally convincing. It was impossible to distinguish them from Cinder, Iko, and Cress.

"Evidently," added the assistant, gaze flashing in Kai's direction, "this all could have been avoided if the ship's mechanic had remembered to bring a pair of *wire cutters.*"

Kai's mouth twitched. That one, then, was Cinder. He tried to imagine her beneath the glamour, smug over her use of their new "code word." He refrained from rolling his eyes at her.

"It's no inconvenience at all," said Kai, focusing on the secretary. "We're glad we could be of assistance. Do you need us to send anyone to retrieve your ship?"

"No, thank you. The Republic has already sent a maintenance crew, but we didn't want to be delayed longer than necessary. We do have a party to get to, you know."

The secretary winked, very un-diplomat-like. Iko, then.

Remembering Cinder's warning—that it would be tiring for her to not only glamour herself but also manipulate the percep-tion of her four comrades, and she didn't know how long she'd be able to maintain it—Kai gestured toward the exit. "Come with me. We have a sitting room where we'll all be comfortable. Can I offer you some tea?"

"I'll have a whiskey on the rocks," said one of the security personnel.

Cinder-the-assistant cast a cold glare at the man. *Thorne.*

"We're fine," said Cinder. "Thank you."

"Right this way." Kai and Torin led their guests away from the docking bay, dismissing the captain and first mate. No one spoke until they'd made their way back to his private rooms.

When Kai faced his guests again, the disguises were gone and the reality of seeing five known criminals in his sitting room reminded him that he'd just put everyone aboard this ship in a great amount of danger.

"Is this room secure?" asked Thorne.

"It should be," said Kai. "We use it for international conferencing and—"

"Cress?"

"On it, Captain." Cress pulled a portscreen from her back pocket and went to the control panel built into the wall, running whatever system check she'd devised.

"This is Konn Torin, my head adviser. Torin, you remember Cin—"

"Wait," said Cinder, holding up a hand.

Kai paused.

Nine long, silent seconds passed between them, before finally Cress unplugged her portscreen. "All clear."

"Thank you, Cress," said Thorne.

Cinder lowered her hand. "Now we can talk."

Kai raised an eyebrow. "Right. Torin, you remember Cinder and Iko."

Torin nodded at them, his arms crossed, and Cinder returned the nod, laced with an equal amount of tension. "I told you I'd return him safely," she said.

A flicker of irony passed over Torin's face. "You promised no harm would come to him. In my opinion, that includes physical injury."

"It was just one punch, Torin." Kai shrugged at Cinder. "I tried to explain it was all a part of the charade."

"I understand perfectly, but forgive me for being defensive." Torin scrutinized their new guests. "Though I'm grateful Kai has been returned, it seems this ordeal is hardly over. I hope you know what you're doing, Linh Cinder."

Kai expected her to make some self-deprecating remark about how Torin wasn't the only one, but instead, after a long silence, Cinder asked, "How much does he know?"

"Everything," said Kai.

She turned back to Torin. "In that case, thank you for your help. May I introduce you to the rest of our team: Iko you've met, and this is our ship's captain, Carswell Thorne, our software engineer, Cress Darnel, and my security officer . . . Wolf."

As Torin greeted their guests with more respect than was required, given the circumstances, Kai's attention lingered on Cinder. She stood ten full paces away from him, and as much as Kai wanted to cross the room and kiss her, he couldn't. Maybe it was Torin's presence. Maybe it was knowing they were on their way to Luna, where he would be married. Maybe he was afraid their time spent on the Rampion had been a dream, too fragile to survive in reality.

Though he'd seen her three days ago, it felt like a lifetime. A wall had been erected between them during that absence, though he wasn't sure what had changed. Their relationship was precarious. Kai felt like if he breathed the wrong way, he might destroy everything, and he could see the same uncertainty mirrored in Cinder's face.

"Oh, look," said Iko, crossing to the row of windows. Luna was emerging in their view, bright white and pocked with a thousand craters and cliffs. They were close enough to see the biodomes, sunlight glinting off their surfaces.

Kai had never in his life dreamed he would step foot on Luna. Seeing it now, the inevitability of his fate made his stomach squeeze tight.

Cinder turned to Kai. She was doing a good job of hiding her anxiety, but he was learning to recognize it beneath her squared shoulders and determined looks. "I hope you have something for us?"

Kai gestured at a cabinet against the wall.

Iko was the first one there, yanking open the doors with effervescent enthusiasm, but it wilted fast when she saw the clothes Nainsi had gathered. The stack was a mix of browns and grays and dull whites, linens and cottons. Simple, utilitarian clothing.

"That looks right," said Wolf, who had been the most helpful in describing what the people of Luna's outer sectors might wear.

While they eyed the clothes and began deciding who got which pieces, Kai crossed to another cabinet and pulled out a sheet of fiberglass android plating and a tub of synthetic skin fibers. "And this is for Iko. Plus everything Cinder should need to install it."

Iko squealed and launched herself across the room. Kai braced himself for another hug, but instead she was all over the new plating, marveling at the supplies. Cinder wasn't far behind.

"These are perfect," said Cinder, examining the fibers. Her eyes glinted teasingly. "You know, if this emperor thing doesn't work out, you might have a future career in espionage."

He gave her a wry look. "Let's make sure this emperor thing works out, all right?"

Cinder's face softened and she smiled for the first time since they'd boarded. Dropping the fibers back into their tub, she hesitated for a moment, before taking the last few steps toward Kai and wrapping her arms around him.

He shut his eyes. Just like that, the wall was gone. His arms were eager to pull her against him.

"Thank you," Cinder whispered, and he knew it wasn't for the clothes or the android parts. The words were weighted with faith and trust and sacrifices Kai wasn't ready to think about just yet. He squeezed her tighter, pressing his temple against her hair.

Cinder was still smiling when she extricated herself from the embrace, though it was laced with determination. "Time is running out," she said. "I suggest we go over the plan, one more time."

Eighteen

WINTER LET THE MAID STYLE HER HAIR, PULLING THE TOP
half into a thick braid threaded with strands of gold and silver
and leaving the rest to cascade around her shoulders. She let the
maid pick out a pale blue dress that grazed her skin like water
and a strand of rhinestones to accent her neck. She let the maid
rub scented oils into her skin.

She did not let the maid put any makeup on her—not even to
cover the scars. The maid didn't put up much of a fight. "I suppose you don't need it, Highness," she said, bobbing a curtsy.

Winter knew she had a sort of exceptional beauty, but she
had never before been given a reason to enhance it. No matter
what she did, gazes would follow her down the corridors. No
matter what she did, her stepmother would snarl and try to hide
her envy.

But since Jacin confessed he was not immune to her appear-
ance, she had been looking forward to this chance to dress up in
new finery. Not that she expected much to come from it other
than a heady satisfaction. She knew it was naïve to think Jacin
might ever do something as crazy as profess his love for her. If he

did love her at all. Which she was confident he did, he *must*, after all these years...yet, his treatment of her had had a distant quality since he joined the royal guard. The professional respect he maintained too often made her want to grab his lapels and kiss *him*, just to see how long it would take for him to thaw.

No, she did not expect a confession or a kiss, and she knew all too well a courtship was out of the question. All she wanted was an admiring smile, one breathless look that would sustain her.

As soon as the maid had gone, Winter peeked into the corridor, where Jacin stood at his post.

"Sir Clay, might I solicit your opinion before we go to greet our Earthen guests?"

He waited two full breaths before responding. "At your service, Your Highness."

He did not, however, remove his attention from the corridor wall.

Smoothing down her skirt, Winter situated herself in front of him. "I wanted to know if you thought I looked sort of pretty today?"

Another breath, this one a bit louder. "Not funny, Princess."

"Funny? It's an honest question." She bunched her lips to one side. "I'm not sure blue is my color."

With a glower, he finally looked at her. "Are you *trying* to drive me crazy?"

She laughed. "Crazy loves company, Sir Clay. I notice you haven't answered my question."

His jaw tightened as he returned his focus to some spot over her head. "Go look for compliments elsewhere, Princess. I'm busy protecting you from unknown threats."

"And what a fine job you're doing." She tried to hide her disappointment as she headed back into her chambers, patting Jacin on the chest as she passed. But with that touch, his hand gathered up a fistful of her skirt, anchoring her beside him. Her heart flipped, and despite all her bravado, Jacin's piercing gaze made her feel tiny and childish.

"Please stop doing this," he whispered, more pleading than angry. "Just . . . leave it alone."

She gulped, and thought to feign ignorance. But, no—ignorance was what she feigned for everyone else. Not Jacin. Never Jacin. "I hate this," she whispered back. "I hate having to pretend like I don't even see you."

His expression softened. "I know you see me. That's all that matters. Right?"

She gave a slight nod, though she wasn't sure she agreed. How lovely it would have been to live in a world where she didn't have to pretend.

Jacin released her and she slipped into her chambers, shutting the door behind her. She was surprised to find herself lightheaded. She must have been holding her breath when he'd stopped her and now—

She froze a few steps into the sitting room. Her gut tightened, her nostrils filling with the iron tang of blood.

It was all around her. On the walls. Dripping from the chandelier. Soaking into the upholstered cushions of the settee.

A whimper escaped her.

It had been weeks since she had one of the visions. None had haunted her since Jacin's return. She'd forgotten the overwhelming dread, the swoop of horror in her stomach.

She squeezed her eyes shut.

"J-Jacin?" Something warm splattered on her shoulder, no doubt staining the beautiful blue silk. She took a step back and felt the area rug squish wetly beneath her feet. "Jacin!"

He burst through the door, and though she kept her eyes pressed tight, she could imagine him behind her, weapon drawn.

"Princess—what is it?" He grabbed her elbow. "Princess?"

"The walls," she whispered.

A beat, followed by a low curse. She heard his gun being replaced in its holster, then he was in front of her, his hands on her shoulders. His voice dropped, becoming tender. "Tell me."

She tried to swallow, but her saliva was thick and metallic. "The walls are bleeding. The chandelier too, and it got on my shoulder, and I think it's staining my shoes, and I can smell it, and taste it, and why—" Her voice unraveled all at once. "Why does the palace hurt so much, Jacin? Why is it always dying?"

He pulled her against him, cradling her body. His arms were stable and protective and he was not bloody and he was not broken. She sank into the embrace, too dazed to return it, but willing to accept the comfort. She buried herself in the security of him.

"Take a breath," he commanded.

She did, though the air was clouded with death.

She was glad to let it out again.

"It's all in your head, Princess. You know that. Say it now."

"It's all in my head," she murmured.

"Are the walls bleeding?"

She shook her head, feeling the press of his ranking pin against her temple. "No. They don't bleed. It's all in my head."

His hold tightened. "You're all right. It will pass. Just keep breathing."

She did. Again and again and again, his voice coaxing her through each breath until the smell of blood gradually subsided.

She felt dizzy and exhausted and sick to her stomach, but glad her breakfast hadn't come up. "It's better now. It's gone."

Jacin exhaled, like he'd been forgetting to breathe himself. Then, in a strange moment of vulnerability, he craned his head and kissed her on the shoulder, right where the nonexistent drop of blood had fallen before. "That wasn't so bad," he said, with a new lightness. "No windows at least."

Winter cringed, remembering the first time she saw the castle walls bleeding. She'd been so distraught and desperate to get away she tried to throw herself from the second-floor balcony—Jacin barely got to her in time to pull her back.

"Or sharp utensils," she said, carrying it off as a joke. The time she'd stabbed a dozen holes into her drapes trying to kill the spiders that were crawling over them, once stabbing her own hand in the process. It had not been a deep wound, but Jacin took care to keep sharp objects away from her ever since.

He pushed to arm's length, inspecting her. She forced a smile, then realized it wasn't forced after all. "It's over. I'm all right."

His eyes warmed and for the briefest of moments she thought—*this is it, this is when he will kiss me*—

There was a cough from the doorway.

Jacin recoiled.

Winter spun around, heart thundering.

Aimery stood in the open door, his expression dark. "Your Highness."

Catching her breath, Winter tucked a curl behind her ear—it must have fallen loose from the braid. She was warm all over. Flustered and nervous and aware that she should be embarrassed, but she was more annoyed at the interruption than anything else.

"Thaumaturge Park," she said with a cordial nod. "I was having one of my nightmares. Sir Clay was assisting me."

"I see," said Aimery. "If the nightmare has receded, I suggest he return to his post."

Jacin clicked his heels and left wordlessly, though it was impossible to tell if it was by his own volition or if Aimery was controlling him.

Still trying to compose herself, Winter fluttered a smile at the thaumaturge. "It must be time to leave for the docks?"

"Nearly," he said, and, to her surprise, he turned and shut the door to the corridor. Her fingers twitched defensively, but not out of concern for herself. Poor Jacin would hate to be left stranded on the other side, unable to protect her should anything happen.

Which was an inane thought. Even if Jacin was present, he could do nothing against a thaumaturge. Winter often thought this was a weakness in their security. She never trusted the thaumaturges, yet they were given so much power within the palace.

After all, a thaumaturge killed her father, and she never got over this fact. To this day, a long sleeve caught from the corner of her eye too often made her startle.

"Was there something you needed?" she asked, trying to appear unconcerned. She was still recovering from the vision. Her stomach was in knots and warm sweat clung to the back of her neck. She wanted to lie down for a minute, but she didn't want to appear any weaker than she already did. Than she already *was*.

"I have come to pose a rather interesting proposition, Your Highness," said Aimery. "One I have been thinking on for some time, and that I hope you will agree is beneficial to us both. I have already suggested the idea to Her Majesty, and she has voiced her approval, on the condition of your consent."

His voice was both slippery and kind. Always when she was in Aimery's presence Winter wished to both cower away and curl up sleepily beneath his steady timbre.

"Forgive me, Aimery, my brain is still muddled from the hallucination and I'm having difficulties understanding you."

His gaze slipped over her, lingering on her scars and on her curves, and Winter was glad she didn't involuntarily shudder.

"Princess Winter Blackburn." He slinked closer. She couldn't resist taking a step back before she managed to stop herself. Fear was a weakness in the court. Much better to act unperturbed. Much safer to act crazy, when in doubt.

She wished she had not told him the nightmare was over. She wished the walls had gone on bleeding.

"You are a darling of the people. Beloved. *Beautiful.*" His fingers stroked beneath her chin, with the delicacy of a feather. This time, she did shudder. "Everyone knows you will never be queen, but that does not mean you cannot wield your own sort of power. An ability to appease the people, to bring them joy. They admire you greatly. It is important that we show the people your support for the royal family and the court that serves them. Don't you agree?"

Her skin had become a mess of goose bumps. "I have always shown support for the queen."

"Certainly you have, my princess." His smile was lovely when he wanted it to be, and the loveliness of it curdled her stomach. Again, he looked at her scars. "But your stepmother and I agree it is time to make a grand statement to the people. A symbolic gesture that shows where you fit into this hierarchy. It is time, Princess, for you to take a husband."

Winter's muscles went taut. She had thought it might be coming to this, but the words in his mouth were repulsive.

She pressed her lips up into a smile. "Of course," she said. "I will be glad to give consideration to my future happiness. I have been told there are many suitors who have posed an interest. As soon as my stepmother's wedding and coronation ceremonies are complete, I'll enjoy looking at the potential suitors and carrying out courtships."

"That will not be necessary."

Her smile was plaster. "What do you mean?"

"I have come to request your hand, Your Highness."

Her lungs convulsed.

"We are perfectly matched. You are beautiful and adored. I am powerful and respected. You are in need of a partner who can protect you with his gift to offset your own disabilities. Think of it. The princess and the queen's head thaumaturge—we will be the greatest envy of the court."

His eyes were shining and it became clear he had been imagining this for a long time. Winter had often thought Aimery might be attracted to her, and this knowledge had been the seed for countless nightmares. She *knew* how he treated the women he was attracted to.

But she had never imagined he would seek a marriage, above the families, above even a potential Earthen arrangement—

No. Now that Levana would be an Earthen empress, it wouldn't matter if Winter could make a match with the blue planet as well. Instead, to marry her weak, pathetic stepdaughter off to a man with such an impressive ability to control the people . . .

It was a smart match, indeed.

Aimery's grin crawled into her skin. "I see I have left you speechless, my princess. Can I take your shock for acquiescence?"

She forced herself to breathe and look away—demure, not disgusted. "I am ... flattered by your offer, Thaumaturge Park. I do not deserve the attentions of one as accomplished as yourself."

"Don't pretend to be coy." He cupped her cheek and she flinched. "Say yes, Princess, and we can announce our engagement at tonight's feast."

She stepped away from his touch. "I am honored, but ... this is so sudden. I need time to consider. I ... I should speak with my stepmother and ... and I think ..."

"Winter." His tone had a new harshness, though his face remained gentle, even impassive. "There is nothing to consider. Her Majesty has approved the union. It is now only your acceptance that is needed to confirm our engagement. Take my offer, Princess. It is the best you will receive."

She glanced at the door, seeking what solace she didn't know. She was trapped.

Aimery's eyes darkened. "I hope you aren't expecting that guard to ask for your hand. I hope you aren't harboring some childish fantasy that to deny *me* is to accept *him*."

She clenched her teeth, smiling around the strain. "Don't be silly, Aimery. Jacin is a dear friend, but I have no intentions toward him."

He scoffed. "The queen would never allow such a marriage."

"I just said—"

"What is your answer? Do not toy with words and meanings, Princess."

Her head swam. She would not—could not—say yes. To Aimery? Cruel, deceitful Aimery, who smiled when there was bloodshed on the throne room floor?

*

But to say no would not do either. She did not care what they might do to her, but if she endangered Jacin with her refusal, if Aimery believed Jacin was the *reason* for her refusal . . .

A knock prolonged her indecision.

Aimery growled, "What?"

Jacin entered, and though he wore no expression, as usual, Winter detected a resentful shade of red on his cheeks.

"Her Highness has been summoned to join the queen's entourage in meeting with our Earthen guests."

Winter crumbled with relief. "Thank you, Sir Clay," she said, skirting around Aimery.

Aimery grabbed her wrist before she was out of reach. Jacin's hand went to his gun, but he didn't draw.

"I will have an answer," Aimery said under his breath.

Winter placed her hand on top of Aimery's, imagining herself unconcerned. "If you must have it now, then I'm afraid the answer must be no," she said, with a flippancy that denied her true feelings. "But give me time to consider your offer, Thaumaturge Park, and perhaps the answer will be different when next we speak of it."

She gave his knuckles a gentle tap and was thankful when he released her.

The look he gave to Jacin as they passed, though, spoke not of jealousy, but murder.

Nineteen

IT TOOK A HEROIC AMOUNT OF EFFORT FOR KAI TO PRETEND
like he wasn't sick with nerves. The ship settled with a thud that
made him jump. Torin's presence beside him, at least, was stabi-
lizing, and he could hear the anxious whispers of the Commonwealth ambassadors as they waited to debark the ship's common
room. He could sense five stowaways hidden aboard the ship—
even though he didn't know where, so there was no chance he
could give their location away with a stray glance.

If anyone was going to draw suspicion, it would be him. Only
he and Torin knew about Cinder and her allies, and Torin's expression was as unperturbed as ever. The ship's crew was too
busy with their arrival procedures to question the disappear-
ance of America's secretary of defense, and none of the other
passengers knew they'd taken guests aboard in the first place.

Whereas Kai couldn't stop thinking about these people—his
friends—and what he was helping them do. Invade Luna. Start a
rebellion. End a war.

He also couldn't stop counting the thousands of things that
could go wrong.

He needed to focus. This would only work if Levana believed Kai was determined to finalize their marriage alliance, once and for all. He had to make her think she had won.

The ramp started to descend. Kai took in a deep breath and held it, trying to clear his mind. Trying to convince *himself* he wanted this marriage and this alliance to succeed.

Artemisia's royal port was glowing up from the floor in a way that immediately made him disconcerted. The walls themselves were rocky and black, but lit with thousands of tiny lights like a starry night sky. The port contained dozens of ships in various sizes, mostly Lunar ships that glimmered uniformly white, painted with unfamiliar runes and displaying the royal seal. Kai also recognized Earthen emblems among the ships—some Earthen guests had already begun to arrive. Seeing them gathered together filled him with dread.

Movement drew his gaze and Kai spotted Levana herself gliding along the wide platform that circled the docks. She was surrounded by her entourage: the ever-smug Head Thaumaturge Aimery Park stood to her right and a girl in a pale blue dress followed behind the queen, her head lowered and her face obstructed by an abundance of curly black hair. There were five additional thaumaturges and at least a dozen more guards. It made for an impressive amount of security—overkill, in Kai's opinion.

Was Levana expecting something to go wrong? Or was this a show of intimidation?

Bracing himself, Kai descended the ramp to meet the queen. His own entourage, including ten of his own guards, followed behind.

"Your Majesty," said Kai, accepting Levana's proffered hand. He bowed to kiss it.

"Always so formal," Levana said in that cloying voice that made his skin crawl. "We cannot refer to each other in such droll terms forever. Perhaps I shall henceforth call you My Beloved, and you shall call me your Sweet."

Kai hovered over her hand, hatred blistering his skin where it touched hers. After a drawn-out moment, he released her and straightened. "*Your Majesty*," he started again, "it is an honor to be welcomed to Luna. My ancestors would have been filled with pride to witness such an occasion."

"The pleasure is my own." Levana's gaze slinked over the ambassadors gathered on the ship's ramp. "I hope you will find our hospitality agreeable. If you need for anything, please let one of the servants know and they will see that you are well taken care of."

"Thank you," said Kai. "We're all curious about the famed luxuries of the white city."

"I've no doubt of it. I'll have some servants brought to unload your belongings and have them taken to your rooms."

"That won't be necessary. Our crew is already unloading the ship." He gestured over his shoulder. A second loading ramp had been lowered out of the cargo bay. He had made sure to tell the captain he wanted the crew to make this a top priority. He wanted to be sure the ship was emptied of both people and cargo as soon as possible, so Cinder and the others wouldn't be trapped in the docks for too long.

"How efficient," Levana said. "In that case, your ambassadors may follow Thaumaturge Lindwurm to our guest suites." She indicated a black-coated man. "I'm sure they would like to rest from such a long journey."

Within moments, Kai's following of nervous companions

were being led to a set of enormous arched doors that glittered with a depiction of a crescent moon over Earth. Though the presence of his Earthen companions had offered no security at all, Kai still felt abandoned as he, Torin, and his guards remained behind.

"I hope you won't think it rude that I didn't offer full introductions to your guests," said Levana. "My stepdaughter is easily distressed, and too many new faces could unnerve her." She floated a hand out to her side, like she was conducting a symphony. "But do allow me to introduce *you*, at least, to my stepdaughter, Princess Winter Hayle-Blackburn of Luna."

"Of course. I've heard so much . . . about . . . you."

Kai trailed off as the princess lifted her head and peered at him through a fringe of thick lashes. It was a brief look, barely a glance, but that was all it took for a rush of heat to climb up Kai's neck and into his ears. He had heard of the princess's legendary beauty. Beauty that was not created by a glamour, they said, unlike Levana's. The rumors weren't exaggerated.

Clearing his throat, Kai forced a composed smile. "I'm honored to meet you, Your Highness."

The princess's eyes were teasing as she stepped beside the queen and lowered into a curtsy with the grace of a dancer. When she rose again, Kai noticed her scars for the first time. Three uniform scars cut down her right cheek. These, too, were legendary, along with the tale of how out of envy Levana had forced the princess to mutilate her own face.

The sight twisted his stomach.

Princess Winter offered him a docile, close-lipped smile. "The honor is mine, Your Imperial Majesty." Drifting closer, she pressed a light kiss to Kai's bruised cheek. His insides turned to goo. He had the presence of mind to be grateful Cinder wasn't witnessing this exchange, because something told him he'd never hear the end of it.

The princess stepped back and he was able to breathe again. "With our introductions complete, I feel it is safe for us to drop any future formalities. After all, with your upcoming nuptials, you're practically my father."

Kai reeled back, his jaw dropping open.

Silent laughter glimmered in the princess's gaze as she took her spot behind her stepmother again. She seemed neither distressed *nor* unnerved.

The queen gave her stepdaughter an annoyed look, before gesturing to the man on her other side. "You will of course remember my head thaumaturge, Aimery Park."

Snapping his mouth shut, Kai inclined his head, though the thaumaturge offered only his signature smugness in return. "Welcome to Luna," he drawled.

Scanning the rest of the entourage, Kai recognized two of the guards too. Seeing the queen's captain of the guard was no surprise, but his teeth clenched when he spotted the blond guard who had been like a shadow to Sybil Mira when she'd been a guest in New Beijing.

Distrust twisted his insides. Cinder had thought this guard was an ally, but she now suspected he'd betrayed them to Sybil when they were trying to make their escape from the palace. His presence here, in uniform again, confirmed her suspicions.

No matter, he thought. Cinder had succeeded, despite his betrayal.

Levana grinned, like she detected the rebelliousness of Kai's thoughts, despite all his attempts to appear complacent. "I believe that leaves only one matter of business to tend to before we show you to your rooms." She snapped her fingers, and two of her thaumaturges and six guards snapped to attention. "Search their ship."

Despite all his attempts at normalcy, Kai couldn't keep away the panic that flared in his chest. "Excuse me?" he said, swiveling his head as the entourage marched past him. "What are you doing?"

"My dear beloved, you didn't think I would blindly trust your word after you've shown so much sympathy to my enemies, did you?" She laced her fingers together. They might have been discussing the weather. "In monitoring your fleet, we noted that you took aboard some passengers from the American Republic, but it seems they're too shy to show themselves."

Kai's stomach sank as one of her guards pulled him and Torin behind the queen, and he was left to watch helplessly as Levana's men boarded his ship. If his own guards thought to offer any protection, they were already under Lunar control.

Kai tightened his fists. "This is absurd. The Americans were with that group you just sent away. There's nothing on that ship but luggage and wedding gifts."

The queen's face hardened. "For your sake, Emperor Kaito, I hope that's true. Because if you came here to betray me, I'm afraid this will be a remarkably unpleasant visit."

Twenty

CINDER WAS PRESSED INTO THE CORNER OF A STORAGE closet, her heart pounding in the darkness. Faint strips of light spilled through the slots in the door, allowing her to make out the profiles and bright eyes of her companions. She could hear the shuffling and thumping as the cargo bay was unloaded beneath their feet.

She tried to think of this like a homecoming. She had been born here—this moon, this city. Here, her birth had been celebrated. Here, she would have been raised to be a queen.

But no matter how she tried to think of it, she did not feel like she was home. She was hiding in a closet with the very real possibility that she would be killed the moment someone recognized her.

She glanced at her companions. Wolf was beside her, jaw tense and brow set in concentration. Against the opposite wall, Iko was crouched down with both hands over her mouth, like the need to be quiet was torture. In the hollow silence, Cinder could detect a subtle hum coming from the android, a hint at the machinery beneath her synthetic skin. Her neck was fixed now—Kai had brought exactly what Cinder needed.

Standing beside Iko, Thorne had one arm draped around Cress's shoulders, his free hand scratching at his jaw. Tucked against him, Cress seemed paler than usual, her anxiety evident even in the darkness.

They were a ragtag group in the drab clothing Kai had brought them, including a black knit hat to cover Iko's blue hair and heavy gloves for Cinder's cyborg hand. Putting them on had dredged up a number of memories. There had been a time when she wore gloves everywhere, when she'd been so ashamed of being cyborg she refused to let her prostheses show. She couldn't recall when that had changed, but now the gloves felt like a lie.

A blue glow drew her attention back to Cress, who had turned on a portscreen and was pulling up a diagram of Artemisia's royal port. "We're in good position," she whispered, tilting the screen to show them. There were three exits from the port— one that led into the palace above them, one that connected to the city's public spaceship docks, and one that led down to the maglev tunnels, which was their destination. The maglev tunnels made up a complex underground transit system, linking all of Luna's sectors together. Cinder had studied the system so many times she would have had it memorized even without having the map downloaded to her brain-machine interface. To her, the system resembled a spiderweb and the capital city of Artemisia was the spider.

Cress was right. The pilots had settled the ship close to the exit that would take them down to the maglev tunnels. It was the best they could have hoped for.

Yet she couldn't deny how tempting it was to abandon the

plan, to forget patience, to try to end it here, now. She was at Levana's doorstep. She was *so close.* Her body was wound up tight, ready to storm the palace—an army of one.

She glanced at Wolf. His fists flexed, in and out, in and out. There was murder in his eyes. *He* would have stormed the palace with her, she knew, in hopes that Scarlet was there. But they didn't even know whether Scarlet was still alive.

But it was desperation goading her, not confidence. Even if she got past Levana's security and somehow managed to kill her, she would end up dead as well. Then some other Lunar would step in to take the throne and Luna would be no better off than it had been before.

She shoved the temptation down into the pit of her stomach. This wasn't about assassinating Levana. This was about giving the citizens of Luna a voice and ensuring it was heard.

She tried to distract herself by going over their plan again in her head. This was the most dangerous part, but she hoped Levana and her security team would be so busy with the arriving Earthen guests they wouldn't notice a handful of dockworkers slipping out of the royal port. Their goal was to make it to Sector RM-9 where they hoped to find Wolf's parents and be offered temporary shelter from which to start the next phase of their plan—informing the people of Luna that their true queen had returned.

If they could make it there undetected, Cinder knew they had a chance.

The clomp of feet startled her. It was too loud—like someone was on the same level as they were, not down below in the cargo bay. She traded frowns with her companions. A distant door was slammed shut and she heard someone yelling orders. More scuffling followed.

"Is it just me," whispered Thorne, "or does it sound like some-one is searching the ship?"

His words mirrored her thoughts exactly. Comprehension turned fast into horror. "She knows we're here. They're looking for us."

She looked around at her companions, their expressions ranging from terrified to eager and all of them, she realized with a start, looking back at her. Awaiting instruction.

Outside their confined closet, the voices grew louder. Something crashed against the floor.

Cinder tightened her gloved fists. "Wolf, Thorne, the second a thaumaturge sees either of you they'll try to control you." She licked her lips. "Do I have permission to take control of you first? Just your bodies, not your minds."

"I've been waiting for you to admit you wanted my body," said Thorne. He laid a hand on the gun at his waist. "Be my guest."

Wolf looked less enthusiastic, but he gave her a sharp nod.

Cinder slipped her will into Thorne as easily as slicing through a block of tofu. Wolf's energy was more chaotic, but she'd spent so much time training with him aboard the Rampion that his energy, too, offered little resistance. Cinder felt their limbs as if they were an extension of her own. Though she knew she was doing it for their own protection, keeping them from being turned into weapons for the enemy, she couldn't help feeling like manipulating them was a betrayal of their trust. It was an unfair balance of power—their safety was now her responsibility.

She thought of Levana, forcing her guard to take a bullet for her at the royal ball, and wondered if she would ever make that same decision with one of her friends.

She hoped she would never have to.

A voice echoed in the nearby corridor: "Nothing in the engine room. You—split up. Search these corridors and report back."

They were close, and if there was a thaumaturge, she knew it wouldn't be long before he or she was near enough to detect the bioelectricity coming from this storage closet. She pictured the ship's layout and tried to formulate a plan, but there was little hope now of slipping away without announcing their presence.

They would have to fight their way out of the ship. They would have to fight all the way to the maglev shuttles.

"Cinder," Thorne whispered. His body was statue still, waiting for Cinder's command. "Send me out there."

Cress's head snapped up, but he didn't return the look.

Cinder frowned. "What?"

"Send me as a decoy, out the main ramp and away from the maglev doors. I'll draw them off long enough for you to get out through the cargo bay."

"Thorne . . ."

"Do it." His eyes flashed. He still wouldn't look at Cress. "We made it to Luna. You don't need a pilot here, or a captain."

Her pulse thundered. "You don't have to—"

Outside someone called, "Press room is clear!"

"Stop wasting time," Thorne said through his teeth. "I'll lead them away and circle back to you."

She knew he was being overconfident, but Cinder found herself nodding at the same time Cress started shaking her head.

"My control of you will be intermittent inside the ship, but if I can find you, I'll reclaim you as soon as we're all outside." *If they don't claim you first,* she thought, unwilling to speak it out loud.

Controlling an Earthen like Thorne was easy, but wresting control away from a thaumaturge was significantly more difficult.

"Got it." Thorne's jaw tensed.

"Be careful," Cress said, more a squeak than a whisper, and Thorne's attention alighted on her for the briefest of moments . . .

Before Cinder kicked open the door and sent Thorne bolting into the corridor. He collided with the wall, but pushed himself off and careened to the left. His arms and legs pumped as he raced toward the main deck. It wasn't long before he was out of her reach. Too much steel divided them. Cinder lost control, and Thorne was on his own.

Seconds after her grasp on him had snapped, they heard a crash. Thorne had broken something.

Cinder hoped it wasn't some priceless Commonwealth artifact.

In the next chamber, a stampede of feet raced after him. When Cinder reached out with her thoughts, she couldn't feel any bioelectricity other than Wolf's. This side of the ship had been cleared.

She tipped her head into the corridor. No sign of anyone aboard. On the other side of the ship, she heard yelling.

Cinder ran in the opposite direction she'd sent Thorne. The others hurried after her—down two levels on a narrow, spiraling stairwell, through an industrial galley that made the kitchen on the Rampion feel like a child's play set, and along a utilitarian corridor dividing the podship docks. They paused above the hatch that would drop them into the cargo bay. Cinder could still hear shuffling and the crank of machinery below, but she had no way of knowing if it was the Earthen workers unloading the cargo, or Lunars inspecting it.

Whoever it was, they didn't have time to wait for them to leave.

Cinder loaded a bullet into her projectile finger. They'd found plenty of ammunition aboard the Rampion, but she couldn't help wishing Kai had been able to procure more tranquilizer darts for her on Earth.

Too late. No time to think.

Wolf popped open the hatch and jumped down first. Cinder once again took control of his body, in case there were Lunars down there, but she had nothing to do with the growl or flash of teeth.

Cinder swung herself down beside him. The floor clanged as Iko dropped next, followed by the tentative thuds of Cress's footsteps on the ladder.

Three figures that had been inspecting the crates swung around to face them. Cinder registered the uniforms of a black-coated thaumaturge and two Lunar guards at the same moment a gun fired.

Her left leg kicked out from under her, the shock wave vibrating up through her hip and into her spine. The bullet had hit her metal thigh.

Cress cried out and froze on the ladder, releasing the rungs only when Iko grabbed her and yanked her off. Cinder urged Wolf's legs to move. They scurried behind a pallet loaded with Commonwealth merchandise just as another bullet pinged on the wall overhead. A third hit the crate, splintering the wood on the other side.

The firing stopped.

Cinder pressed her back to the crate, reorienting herself. She stretched out her thoughts, finding the Lunars' bioelectricity sizzling in the room, but of course the guards were already under the thaumaturge's control.

The ramp that would let them escape from the ship was on the opposite side of the cargo bay.

Eerie silence fell, leaving Cinder jumpy as she strained to listen for footsteps coming toward them. She expected the Lunars would try to surround them. Their weapons wouldn't stay quiet for long.

Wolf's limbs were still for once, and it occurred to Cinder that *she* was holding him so still. Only his expression was alive. Fierce, wild. He was her best weapon, but under her control he would be clunky and awkward—not half as brutal as he could be on his own. Their training aboard the Rampion had focused on stopping an enemy. Disarming them. Removing a threat.

She wished now they would have spent more time practicing how to turn people into weapons. It was a skill that Levana and her minions excelled at.

Wolf met her gaze, and a thought occurred to her. Cinder was controlling his body, but not his mind or his emotions. What if she changed tactics? She could still protect him from the thaumaturge's power while allowing him to do what he did best.

"Get the thaumaturge," she whispered, then released Wolf's body and snatched at his thoughts instead. She fed him a vision of the first terrible thing that came to mind: the fight aboard the Rampion between them and Sybil Mira. The day Scarlet had been taken.

Wolf vaulted over the crate. Gunshots blared, bullets pinged, the walls shook.

Iko roared and launched herself past Cinder, tackling a guard who appeared in the corner of Cinder's vision. His gun fired; the bullet struck the ceiling. Iko punched him and his head cracked against the metal floor. His body stopped flailing, unconscious.

Cinder jumped to her feet, holding her cyborg hand like a gun, and spotted the second guard creeping around to their other side. His face was blank—unafraid. Then, as she watched, it cleared. His eyes focused on Cinder, bewildered.

The thaumaturge had lost control of him.

The moment was fleeting. The guard snarled and aimed his gun at Cinder, but he was too late. Already she had a grip on his bioelectricity. With a thought, she sent him spiraling into unconsciousness. He dropped to his knees and collapsed face-first to the floor with a crunch. Blood spurted from his nose. Cinder recoiled.

A scream echoed through the bay.

Cinder could no longer see Wolf, and terror struck her. In taking control of the guard, she'd forgotten about protecting Wolf's mind from—

The screaming stopped, followed by a thud.

A second later, Wolf appeared from behind a shelf stacked with suitcases, snarling and shaking out his right fist.

Pulse thrumming, Cinder turned to see Iko with her arm wrapped around an extra-pale Cress.

They ran for the ramp, and Cinder was grateful that it was lowered to face away from the palace entrance. As they crept downward, she scanned their surroundings, with both her eyes and her Lunar gift. In this wide-open space, she could sense a cluster of people in the distance and she could tell there were both Earthens and Lunars in the mix.

Their route to the maglev doors, at least, was unblocked. If they were careful, they could stay hidden behind this row of ships.

At least, until one of those Lunars picked up on Wolf's sizzling energy and questioned what a modified soldier was doing here.

She waved her arm and they skimmed around the side of the ramp. A breath passed while Cinder waited for a sign they'd been noticed. When none came, they darted to the next ship, and the next. Every thump of their feet pounded in her ears. Every breath sounded like a windstorm.

A shout startled her and together they ducked behind the landing gear of an elaborately painted ship from the African Union. Cinder held her hand at the ready, the bullet still loaded in her finger.

"Over there!" someone yelled.

Cinder peered around the telescoping legs of the spacecraft and spotted a figure bolting between ships. Thorne, running away from them at full speed.

Not yet controlled by a Lunar.

Heart leaping, Cinder reached out for his mind, hoping to get to him before one of the Lunars on the other side of the dock . . .

Success.

Like with Wolf, she thrust an idea into his head.

Get back here.

Startled, Thorne tripped and fell, rolled a couple times, and sprang again to his feet. Cinder flinched with guilt, but was relieved when Thorne changed directions. He skirted around a couple podships, dodging a volley of bullets from a cluster of guards that had emerged from the main ramp of Kai's ship.

"I've got him," said Cinder. "Come on."

Keeping half her focus on Thorne, the rest on her own careful movements, Cinder stayed close to Wolf as they ducked in and out of the safety of the spacecraft, weaving their way to the wide platform that stood shoulder height around the perimeter of the docks. Their exit loomed before them. Enormous double doors carved in mysterious Lunar runes. A sign above them indicated the way to the maglev platform.

They reached the last ship. They'd run out of shelter. Once they were on the platform, they would be on raised, wide-open ground.

Cinder glanced back. Thorne was on his stomach beneath the tail of a solo-pilot pod. He waved at them to go ahead, to hurry.

"Iko, you and Cress go first," said Cinder. If they were seen, they at least couldn't be manipulated. "We'll cover you."

Iko put herself between Cress and the palace doors and they ran for the short flight of steps. Cinder swung her embedded gun from side to side, searching for threats, but the guards were too focused on finding Thorne to notice them.

A hiss drew her attention back to the platform. Iko and Cress were at the doors, but they were still shut.

Cinder's stomach dropped.

They were supposed to open automatically.

But—no. Levana had been expecting them. Of course she had taken precautions to ensure they wouldn't be able to escape.

Her face contorted, desperation crashing into her. She struggled to come up with another way out. Would Wolf be strong enough to pry open the doors? Could they fire their way through?

As she racked her brain, a new expression came over Cress, replacing her wide-eyed terror with resolve. Cinder followed her gaze to a circular control booth that stood between the maglev and palace entrances. Before Cinder could guess her plan, Cress had dropped to her hands and knees and started crawling along the wall.

A gun fired. Cress flinched but kept going.

It was followed by another shot, and another, each making Cinder duck down farther. With the third shot there was a shatter of glass.

Cinder spun around, her heart in her throat, and sought out Thorne. He hadn't moved, but now he was holding a handgun, and had it aimed behind him. He'd shot out a window on Kai's ship.

He was causing another distraction, trying to draw more attention to himself, to keep it away from Cress.

Throat dry as desert sand, Cinder looked back to see that Cress had made it to the booth. She was clutching her portscreen, the fingers of her other hand dancing over an invisi-screen. Iko was still by the doors, crouched into a ball, ready to spring up and run at the slightest provocation.

Beside Cinder, Wolf was focused on Thorne, ready to rush into the fight the second one broke out.

Footsteps came pounding down the ramp of Kai's ship and additional Lunar guards swarmed the aisles. It wasn't the guards that concerned Cinder, though. They wouldn't be skilled enough to detect Thorne in their midst. It was their thaumaturges that worried her, but she couldn't find them.

Doors whistled. Wolf grabbed Cinder's elbow before she could turn around and dragged her up to the platform.

Cress had gotten the doors open.

Iko was already on the other side, her back against a corridor wall, waving them on. She had drawn her own gun for the first time and was searching for a target.

"There!"

Wolf and Cinder pounded up the stairs. A bullet pinged against the wall, and she ducked and stumbled through the doors. They slammed into the wall beside Iko.

Cinder looked back, panting. Their pursuers had given up trying to catch them off guard and were now running toward them at full speed. But Thorne had a head start, and he, too, had given up secrecy for speed. Cinder fed images into his mind—his legs running fast as a gazelle's, his feet barely touching the ground. She was too afraid that to turn him into a puppet would only slow him down, but the mental encouragement seemed to work. His speed increased. He bounded up the stairs in two steps.

Over his shoulder, Cinder finally saw the thaumaturge, a woman with short black hair and a red coat.

Gritting her teeth, she raised her arm and fired. She didn't know where she'd hit her, but the woman cried out and fell.

Thorne threw himself across the threshold as the guards reached the base of the platform steps. The doors slammed shut behind him.

Thorne collapsed against the wall, holding his chest. His cheeks were flushed, but his eyes were bright with adrenaline as he looked around at the group. At Cinder, at Iko, at Wolf.

The growing smile vanished. "Cress?"

Cinder, still gasping for her own breath, shook her head.

His jaw fell slack with horror. He pushed himself off the wall and lunged for the doors, but Wolf jumped in front of him, pinning Thorne's arms to his sides.

"Let me go," Thorne growled.

"We can't go back," said Wolf. "It's suicide."

To punctuate his words, a volley of bullets struck the doors, their loud clangs echoing down the corridor they were now trapped in.

"We're not leaving her."

"Thorne—" started Cinder.

"No!" Wriggling one arm free, Thorne swung, but Wolf

ducked. In half a heartbeat, Wolf had spun around and pinned Thorne to the wall, one enormous hand at Thorne's throat.

"She gave us this chance," Wolf said. "Don't waste it."

Thorne's jaw flexed. His body was taut as a cable, ready to fight, though he was no match for Wolf. Panic was etched into every line of his face, but slowly, slowly, his erratic breaths started to even.

"We have to go," said Cinder, almost afraid to suggest it.

Thorne's focus shifted to the closed doors.

"I could stay?" suggested Iko, her tone uncertain. "I could go back for her?"

"No," said Cinder. "We stay together."

Thorne flinched and Cinder realized the cruelty of her words too late. Their group was already divided.

She inched forward to settle a hand on Thorne's arm, but thought better of it. "We'd still be out there if it wasn't for her. We'd *all* be captured, but thanks to Cress, we're not. She saved us. Now, we have to *go*."

He squeezed his eyes. His shoulders slumped.

His whole body was trembling, but he nodded.

Wolf released him and they ran.

BOOK
Two

The huntsman took pity on her and said,

"Run away into the woods, child, and never come back."

Twenty-One

AT SOME POINT DURING THE EXCITEMENT FOLLOWING Emperor Kaito's arrival, Jacin had placed himself in front of Winter—ever her protector—and she gathered up the back of his shirt's material in one fist. His presence was part comfort, part annoyance. He kept blocking her view.

Her sight was clear as daybreak, though, as she watched four figures dash through the exit that led down to the maglev shuttles. The doors slammed shut to a volley of gunfire. Though they had been too far away to see clearly, Winter was certain one of them was Linh Cinder.

Her dear missing cousin, Princess Selene.

"Follow them!" Levana shouted. The guards who had been sent to search the emperor's ship were at the exit within seconds, trying to pry the doors open, but they wouldn't budge.

Levana wheeled around to face Sir Jerrico Solis. "Send one team through the palace to the lakeside entrances, another through the city. Try to cut them off at the platform."

Jerrico clasped a hand to his fist and was gone, summoning eight other guards to follow.

"Aimery," Levana barked, "see to it that all shuttles leaving Artemisia are stopped. Have them searched, along with all connecting tunnels and platforms. They are not to make it out of the city. And find out how they were able to get through those doors!"

Aimery bowed. "I have already summoned the technician. We will have the entire system locked down."

Nostrils flaring, Levana straightened her spine and turned to face the emperor. He was standing near the back of their small group—alone, but for a handful of Earthen guards and his adviser. Yet he didn't look afraid. Winter thought he should have looked afraid, but his lips were pressed together in a strained effort not to smile.

Winter cocked her head, inspecting him. He seemed proud. Borderline smug. She began to feel guilty for having teased him before.

"Stowaways," he said, once he had Levana's attention. His shoulders twitched in an unconcerned shrug. "What an unexpected surprise."

Levana's face was fiercely beautiful. Breathtaking in her viciousness. "You have brought a known enemy into the heart of my country. In a time of mutual cease-fire, you have committed an act of treason."

Kai didn't flinch. "My loyalty lies with the Eastern Commonwealth and with Earth. Not with Luna, and certainly not with you."

Levana's eyes narrowed. "You seem confident that I won't have you killed for this."

"You won't," he said with, as her stepmother guessed, an overabundance of confidence. Winter squirmed, suddenly afraid for him. "At least," Kai amended, "not yet."

One perfect eyebrow lifted. "You're right," said Levana. "Perhaps I will kill your adviser instead. Surely he was aware of this blatant betrayal of my trust."

"Do with me as you see fit," said the adviser, as unshaken as Kaito. "*My* loyalties lie only with my emperor."

Kai's cheek twitched. "If you harm any one of your Earthen guests as either a punishment or a threat to me, I will refuse to continue with this wedding."

"Then I will no longer have any reason to keep you alive."

"I know," said Kai, "but you also won't get to be empress."

Their gazes warred with each other while Winter, Jacin, and the other guards watched. Winter's heartbeat was erratic as she waited for the queen's order to have Emperor Kaito killed—for his insolence as much as for his role in bringing Linh Cinder to Artemisia.

The doors to the palace opened and a guard entered, escorting one of their technicians.

"My Queen, you summoned?"

Aimery stepped forward. "There had been strict orders that the exits out of this port were to be locked, but it seems there has been a malfunction. Her Majesty demands to know what went wrong, and be assured it won't happen again."

The technician bowed and scurried around the platform toward the control panel that monitored the exits and the massive spaceship-holding chamber beyond the port doors.

Winter was watching him when her eye caught on a slip of movement. She frowned, sure she saw someone ducking in between some of the Earthen cargo.

Or as sure as she could be of anything she saw, which was not very sure at all.

Her stepmother rounded again on the emperor and flicked

her arm toward him, irritated with his presence. "Take the Earthens to their quarters," she said, "and keep them there."

The emperor and his entourage put up no resistance as the guards shuffled them away with more force than was necessary. Kai didn't look in Winter's direction, but as he passed she could see he was no longer hiding his grin. He might have become a prisoner of the queen, but clearly he saw this as a victory.

The guards' clomping footsteps had faded when the technician shouted, "My Queen!" His fingers were dancing over the screens, his face set with panic. Levana swept toward him. The rest of her entourage trailed after, and though Jacin moved to keep himself in front of Winter, she dodged around him and skipped ahead, ignoring his low growl. She scanned the stacks of crates and luggage again, but there was no sign of the mysterious figure she'd imagined before.

"What?" Levana snapped.

The technician didn't turn away from the controls. On the nearest screen, Winter could see a map of the shuttle system and a flashing error message in the corner. Jacin appeared again at her side and cast her a cool glare for leaving the circle of his protection. She ignored him.

"It's—" the technician started. He swiveled to another screen.

"I suggest you find your tongue before I disable it permanently," said Levana.

The technician shuddered and turned back to face them, though his hands lingered uselessly over the screens. "The system is . . ."

Levana waited.

Winter became very worried for this man's life.

". . . inaccessible, My Queen. I can't . . . I can't access the shuttle schedules, the manual overrides . . . even the entrances to the main platform have been locked. With . . . with the exception of the corridor connecting it to these docks, which alone was left unimpeded."

Levana, lips pressed into a firm line, said nothing.

"The system has been hacked?" said Aimery.

"Y-yes, I think so. It could take hours to reconfigure the access codes . . . I don't even know what they *did*."

"Are you telling me," said Levana, "that you cannot even put a stop to the shuttles leaving the city?"

The technician had gone pale. "I will keep trying, Your Majesty. I'll have much better access to the system from the palace control room, so I'll just—"

"Do you have an apprentice?" said the queen. "Or a partner in your trade?"

The hair stood up on Winter's neck.

The technician stammered, "Th-there are three of us . . . here in the palace . . . but I have the most experience, with over twenty years of loyal service and—"

"Kill him."

A guard removed the gun from his holster. Winter turned her head away, and though it was a petty thought, she was glad it wasn't Jacin being forced to do the murder. If he had still been guard to the head thaumaturge, it very well could have been.

"Please, My Que—"

Winter jumped as the shot rang through her head, followed by a sound she was all too familiar with. A whimper. Coming from behind a stack of cargo bins.

Behind her, the crackle of wiring and splinter of plastic suggested the bullet had struck one of the screens as well. The guard holstered his gun.

Aimery turned to the queen. "I will contact Jerrico and see if his teams have managed to gain access to the platform, and alert him that their way may be impeded."

"Thank you, Aimery. Also alert the other two technicians to the problem with the shuttle system."

Aimery pulled out his portscreen and stepped away from their group, toward the edge of the platform. He was overlooking the piled cargo crates, and though his attention was on his port, Winter was searching for another sign of life below.

There. A foot, she thought, curling in against a large trunk.

Winter gasped delightedly and laced her fingers beneath her chin. Everyone spun to her, startled at her presence, which was not uncommon. "Do you think the Earthens brought us gifts, Stepmother?"

Without waiting for a response, she lifted her skirts and trotted toward the cargo, climbing over the uneven stacks of crates and bins until she reached the lower level.

"Winter," Levana snapped. "What are you doing?"

"Looking for presents!" she called back, giggling. Jacin's shadow fell over her from above. She could picture his expression down to the annoyed twitch in his brow, and she knew that from where he stood with the rest of the queen's entourage, he could not see what she was seeing.

A girl with cropped blonde hair and terrified blue eyes was curled into a tight ball. Her back was pressed up against a crate, her whole body trembling.

Winter lifted her head and beamed, first at Jacin, then her stepmother, doing her best not to look at the spray of blood on the far wall. "This one says it has wine from Argentina! It must be from the Americans. We can toast to such an eventful afternoon."

She leaned over the shaking girl and unlatched the crate with a loud clack. She pried up the lid. "Oh, drat, the box lied. It's only packing fluff." Holding the lid with one hand, she started pulling out the shredded paper as quickly as she could, scattering it over the floor at her feet. The girl gawked up at her.

Her stepmother's voice had turned to ice. "Sir Clay, please escort your charge from the premises. She is embarrassing herself."

Her words carried too much weight, but Winter didn't try to decipher them. She was busy nudging at the girl with her toe, gesturing for her to get into the crate.

Jacin's boots thumped against the cargo as he descended toward her. Winter grabbed the girl's elbow and tugged, spurring the girl into action. She scrambled onto her knees, gripped the edge of the crate, and hauled herself inside—the noise muffled by Winter's crumpling of the paper.

Without waiting to see whether the girl was comfortable, Winter dropped the lid shut as Jacin dropped down beside her. Her grin brightened at him. "Oh, good, you're here! You can help me carry this paper up to my room. What a thoughtful gift from the Americans, don't you think?"

"Princess—"

"I agree, Jacin. A box full of paper is a bit messy for a wedding gift, but we shan't be ungrateful." She scooped up an armful of the paper and pranced toward the palace entrance, not once daring to look back.

Twenty-Two

CINDER WAS USED TO SENSING WOLF'S ENERGY—TIRELESS and agitated and steaming off him like heat waves over pavement. But it was a new thing coming from Thorne, who was normally unshakable. As they ran down an endless staircase, deeper and deeper into Luna's underground, Thorne's energy was every bit as palpable as Wolf's. Angry, terrified, burdened with guilt. Cinder wished she could turn off her Lunar gift so she wouldn't have to deal with her companions' tirade of emotions in addition to her own.

They'd lost Cress. Levana knew of Kai's betrayal. Already their group was fragmented and her plan was falling to pieces.

The steps leveled off into a long, narrow corridor lined with robed statues, each holding a glowing orb that cast swells of light onto the arched ceiling. The floor was fitted with thousands of tiny black and gold tiles, creating a pattern that swirled and ebbed like the Milky Way. It would have been a marvel to behold if they had the time to appreciate it, but Cinder's thoughts were too tumultuous. Listening for sounds of pursuit. Picturing Cress's face, determined in spite of her fear. Trying to plan their next move, and what they would do if the maglevs failed—for Levana must know where they were heading.

At the end of the corridor they came to another spiraling staircase carved from dark, polished wood. The rails and steps were undulating and uneven, and it took Cinder two flights—gripping the rails to keep from falling headfirst in her hurry—to realize the staircase was carved to resemble an enormous octopus that was allowing them passage on its looping tentacles.

So beautiful. So strange. Everything made with such striking craftsmanship and detail. And all this in just some tunnels hundreds of feet beneath the moon's surface. She couldn't imagine how stunning the palace itself must be.

They reached another set of double doors inset with an artfully rendered map showing the entirety of the maglev system.

"This is the platform," said Iko, the only one of them not panting.

"I'll go out first," said Cinder. "If anyone is out there, I'll use a glamour to make them see us as members of Levana's court. Any thaumaturges we kill on sight. Everyone else we ignore."

"What about guards?" said Iko.

"Guards are easy to control. Let me deal with them." She adjusted the scratchy gloves Kai had given her, then opened her thoughts, prepared to detect the bioelectricity off anyone who might have been on the platform. She pressed her palm against the doors. At her touch, they divided into four sections that spiraled into the walls. Cinder stepped onto the platform.

Empty.

She couldn't imagine it would be that way for long.

Three shimmering white shuttles waited on the rails. They ran for the first one. Cinder let the others climb in first, ready to call up a glamour at the first sign of someone approaching, but the platform remained silent. Wolf grabbed Cinder and dragged her in with them.

"How do we work this thing?" Iko cried, pounding at the control screen. The shuttle remained open and motionless. "Shut door! Move! Get us out of here!"

"It won't work for you," said Wolf, leaning past Iko to press all five fingertips against the screen. It lit up and the doors glided shut.

It was a false sense of protection, but Cinder couldn't help a breath of relief.

A tranquil voice filled the shuttle. "Welcome, Alpha Ze'ev Kesley, Lunar Special Operative Number 962. Where shall I take you?"

He glanced at Cinder.

She stared at the screen, sifting through the possibilities. Giving directions to RM-9 was a sure way of leading Levana straight to them. She pulled up the map of Luna on her retina display, trying to strategize the best route, one that would lead Levana off their track.

"WS-1," said Thorne. He was slumped on the floor between the two upholstered benches, his hands draped over his knees, his head against the wall. Between the disheartened expression and collapsed posture, he was almost unrecognizable. But at his voice, the shuttle rose up on the magnetic force beneath the rails and started racing away from Artemisia.

"Waste salvage?" Iko said.

Thorne shrugged. "I thought it would be good to have a Plan B in case something like this happened."

After a short silence, in which Iko's internal workings hummed, she said, "And Plan B is to go to the waste salvage sector?"

Thorne looked up. His voice was neutral as he explained, "It's a short trip from Artemisia, so we won't be giving Levana too much time to regroup and send people after us before we get out of this shuttle. And it's one of the most connected sectors on Luna, given that everyone has waste. There are fifteen maglev tunnels branching out from that one platform. We can go on foot for a ways, throw them off our course, then start doub—"

"Don't say it," said Cinder. "We don't know if we'll be recorded in here."

Thorne shut his mouth and nodded.

Cinder knew he'd been about to say they could start doubling back toward RM-9. She focused in on sector WS-1 on the map in her head, and Thorne was right. It was a smart plan. She couldn't believe she hadn't thought of it herself. "Good call, Thorne."

He shrugged again, without enthusiasm. "Criminal master-mind, remember?"

Cinder sagged onto the bench beside Wolf, allowing her body a brief respite from the pumping adrenaline. "The system recognized you."

"Every Lunar citizen is in the database. I've only been missing for a couple of months—I figured they wouldn't have had my identity removed yet."

"Do you think they'll notice if a special operative who's sup-posed to be on Earth suddenly shows up again?"

"I don't know. But as long as we're traveling by shuttle, using my identity will draw less attention than yours. And without Cress here to break into it . . ."

Thorne flinched and pressed his forehead into the shuttle wall. They sat in silence for a long time, the lack of Cress's pres-ence filling up the hollow spaces around them.

Only in her absence did Cinder realize how much they'd been

relying on Cress. She could have sneaked them through the mag-lev system without having to input any identities. And Cress had been confident that, once they arrived in RM-9, she could disable any surveillance equipment that might give them away. Plus there was the all-important matter of infiltrating Luna's broadcasting system to share Cinder's message with Luna's citizens.

But knowing how much Cress's loss impacted their objectives was nothing compared to the horror Cinder felt. Cress would be tortured for information on their whereabouts and then almost certainly killed.

"She's a shell," Cinder said. "They can't detect her bioelectricity. As long as she stays hidden, she'll be—"

"Don't," said Thorne.

Cinder stared at his whitened knuckles and struggled for something meaningful to say. Her grand plan of revolution and change had just begun and already she felt like a failure. This seemed worse than failing the people of Luna, though. She'd failed the people she cared about most in the universe.

Finally, she whispered, "I'm so sorry, Thorne."

"Yeah," he said. "Me too."

Twenty-Three

JACIN WAS EXTRA BROODY AS WINTER LED HIM INTO THE
elevator.

"Why do I have a bad feeling about this?" he grumbled, eyeing
Winter suspiciously.

"You have a bad feeling about *everything*," she said, nudging
him with her shoulder. It was a playful gesture, one that always
made her giddy to have returned. This time, it was not returned.
She frowned. "I forgot something down in the ports. It will only
take a moment."

She fluttered her lashes at him.

He scowled and looked away. He was in guard mode. Uniform. Posture. Inability to hold eye contact for more than half a
second.

Guard Jacin was not her favorite Jacin, but she knew it was
only a disguise, and one that was forced upon him.

She was itching to tell him the truth from the instant they'd
left the ports. She was stricken with anxiety over the fate of the
girl she'd ushered into that crate. Was she still in hiding? Did she

try to run and rejoin her friends? Had she been found? Captured? Killed?

This girl was an ally of Linh Cinder's, and perhaps a friend of her Scarlet's as well. Fear for her life turned Winter into a pacing, fidgety mess for the two hours that she'd forced herself to wait in her chambers, so as not to draw attention to her return to the docks. Her awareness of the palace surveillance system kept her from telling the secret to even Jacin. It had been a difficult secret to retain.

But if she'd been acting odd, even Jacin didn't ask her about it. No doubt the day's excitement was plenty reason enough for her agitation.

"What was it?" Jacin asked.

Winter peeled her focus from the descending indicator above the elevator door. "Pardon?"

"What did you forget in the ports?"

"Oh. You'll see."

"Princess—"

The doors swished open. She grabbed his arm and pulled him through the lavish gallery where Artemisians could await their transport. This level was abandoned, just as she'd hoped. Though it had been easy for Winter to gain access to the ports from the guard in the palace above—it had taken little more than a pout and defiantly ignoring Jacin's groan—the ports were supposed to be off-limits for the duration of the Earthens' visit. *For the security of their ships and belongings,* Levana had said, but Winter knew it was really to prevent anyone from trying to leave.

The ports were quiet when they stepped onto the main platform. The glowing floor made the ships' shadows appear monstrous on the high ceilings, and the cavernous walls echoed every footstep, every breath. Winter imagined she could hear her own thunderous heartbeat ricocheting back to her.

She took off around the platform with Jacin following at a fast clip. She couldn't help glancing toward the control booth, and though there remained a broken screen and a few dark stains on the wall, the technician's body was gone. To her knowledge, his replacements were still in the palace's main control center trying to regain access to the malfunctioning system.

Her attention swept down to the lower level and endless relief filled her to see the cargo untouched. Though the ambassadors' personal luggage had been taken to their suites, their gifts and trade goods had been left behind for retrieval at a later date.

Winter spotted the box of Argentinian wine. Her pace quickened.

"Stars above," Jacin grumbled. "If you dragged me down here for more packing paper—"

"*Paper*," said Winter, scrambling unladylike over the cargo boxes, "is a most difficult resource to obtain. The lumber sectors have enough demand for building supplies. I once had to trade a pair of silk slippers for half a dozen greeting cards, you know."

It was only partly true. Most of the paper goods available in Artemisia's shops were made from pulped bamboo, which was one of the few resources that grew with abundance in the agriculture sectors. But bamboo also contributed to textile and furniture manufacturing, and even that paper was in limited supply.

Winter was fond of paper. She liked the crisp, tactile way it crinkled beneath her fingers.

Jacin sat down on a plastic bin, his legs dangling over the edge. In the serene solitude of the docks, Guard Jacin had withdrawn. "You want to turn packing paper into greeting cards?"

"Oh, no," she said. "I have no interest in the paper."

One eyebrow rose. "The wine, then?"

Winter unlatched the shipping crate. "Not the wine, either."

She held her breath and heaved open the lid. It clattered against the next bin and Winter found herself staring into a large shipping crate with a layer of tight-packed wine bottles and loose bits of paper and no sign of the girl.

Her heart plummeted.

"What?" Jacin leaned forward to peer into the box. His face took on a layer of concern. "Princess?"

Her lips parted, then snapped shut again. She turned in a slow circle, examining the crates stacked all around her. The girl could have sneaked into any of them.

Or she could have run.

Or she could already have been found by someone else.

Jacin dropped down from his perch and grabbed her elbow. "What's wrong?"

"She's gone," Winter murmured.

"*She?*"

"There was—" She hesitated. Her gaze darted up to one of the many inconspicuous cameras along the dock's perimeter. Though the queen would have demanded them to be disabled while she was there, Winter had no idea if or when they'd been reinstated.

Jacin bristled, with impatience but also worry. Checking for the cameras was the first sign someone was going against the queen's wishes. After a quick sweep of the ceiling, he shook his head. "No indicator lights. They're still off." He was frowning as he said it, though. "Tell me what's going on."

Winter swallowed. "There was a girl. I think she came with Linh Cinder and her companions. I saw her sneaking around these crates while the queen was arguing with the technician, so I hid her in here. But . . . now she's gone."

Jacin rocked back on his heels. Winter expected him to chastise her for doing something so dangerous and right in front of the queen, no less. But instead, after a long hesitation, he asked, "What did she look like?"

"Small. Short blonde hair. Afraid." Remembering the girl's terrified expression made Winter shiver. "Maybe she tried to rejoin her companions. Or . . . or maybe she's back on the emperor's ship?"

Jacin's gaze had unfocused. "Cress," he whispered, turning around. He released Winter's elbow and bounded back up the crates, vaulting onto the platform overhead.

"What? Jacin?" She lifted her skirt over her knees and hurried after him. By the time she'd managed to get back up onto the platform, Jacin was in the control booth, yanking open cabinets filled with wires and cords and computer parts that Winter didn't comprehend.

He found the girl behind the third door he opened, her body curled into such a tight ball Winter couldn't believe she hadn't suffocated. Her wide eyes attached to Jacin and widened, impossibly, further.

Winter staggered to a halt as Jacin reached into the cabinet and pulled the girl out. The girl yelped, trying to regain her footing as Jacin shoved the door shut behind her. She pried her arm out of his grip and backed against the wall, trembling like a caged animal.

Rather than reaching for her again, Jacin took a step back and pinched the bridge of his nose. He cursed. "Princess, you have got to stop collecting these rebels."

Ignoring him, Winter drifted toward the girl, her hands placating. "We won't hurt you," she cooed. "It's all right."

The girl spared her a hasty glance before turning back to Jacin. Terrified, but also angry.

"My name is Winter," she said. "Are you hurt?"

"We can't stay here," said Jacin. "The cameras will be coming on again any minute. It's a miracle they haven't already."

The girl continued to stare at him with her timid ferocity.

"Wait." Jacin laughed. "You disabled them, didn't you?"

The girl said nothing.

Winter swiveled her attention from her to Jacin. "*She* disabled them?"

"This girl used to be the queen's best-kept secret. She can find her way around any computer system." He crossed his arms, his stern expression softening into an almost smile. "You're the one who's been messing with the shuttles too."

The girl's lips thinned into a line.

"What's your name?" asked Winter.

When the girl still didn't respond, Jacin answered, "Her name is Cress. She's a shell and one of Linh Cinder's allies." He scratched his temple. "I don't suppose you have a plan as to what we're supposed to do with her?"

"We could sneak her up to the guest wing? I'm sure the Earthen emperor would watch over her. He did help them get here, after all."

Jacin shook his head. "He's under too much security. We'd never get her close. Besides, the fewer people who know you helped her, the less chance of Levana finding out."

The girl—Cress—seemed to be relaxing as it became apparent Winter and Jacin weren't going to have her executed. Winter smiled at her. "I've never met a shell before. What a marvelous gift. I can't sense you at all, like you're not even there, even though you're standing right in front of me." Her grin broadened. "That would drive my stepmother mad."

"It *was* a shell who killed the last king and queen," said Jacin. "Maybe we can turn her into an assassin."

Winter turned to him, aghast. "Does she *look* like an assassin?"

He shrugged. "Does she look like she's capable of disabling our entire maglev system?"

"I didn't disable it." Cress's voice was meek, but Winter was so surprised to hear her speak, she might as well have shouted. "I changed the access parameters so the queen couldn't shut it down."

Jacin stared at her. "But you could disable it, if you wanted to."

After a beat, the girl dropped her gaze to the floor.

"We have to find someplace to keep her," said Winter, tugging on a curl of hair. "Somewhere safe."

"Why?" said Cress. "Why are you helping me?"

Winter didn't know if she was asking her or Jacin, but Jacin answered first with a grumbled "Good question."

Winter shoved him hard in the shoulder. He barely shifted.

"Because it's the right thing to do. We're going to protect you. Aren't we, Jacin?"

When Jacin said nothing, Winter shoved him again. "Aren't we?"

Jacin sighed. "I think we can sneak her into the guard quarters. It's not far and we won't have to go into the main part of the castle."

With obvious disbelief, Cress said, "*You're* going to protect me?"

"Rather against my will," said Jacin, "but it looks like it."

"For as long as we can," said Winter. "And, if the opportunity arises, we'll do our best to reunite you with your friends."

For the first time, Cress's defenses began to slip. "They got away?"

"It would seem so. They haven't been found yet, as far as I can tell."

"But the queen won't stop looking," added Jacin, as if either of them weren't aware.

Cress had stopped trembling. Her expression became thoughtful as she stared at Jacin. Finally, she asked, "I don't suppose the guard quarters have access to the royal broadcasting network?"

Twenty-four

THEIR PROGRESS THROUGH LUNA'S OUTER SECTORS WAS
slow and tedious. Sometimes taking maglev shuttles, sometimes
walking through the tunnels, sometimes using Wolf's identity to
send a shuttle on without them before skipping to a different
platform and heading in the opposite direction. Sometimes they
split up and rejoined one another a couple of sectors over, to
confuse any security personnel looking for a group of two men
and two women traveling together.

They kept their heads down. Iko kept her hair hidden beneath her cap. Cinder fidgeted with her gloves to be sure her
metal hand wouldn't be seen on any of the cameras. Though
they avoided what surveillance cameras they could, she knew
they couldn't miss them all. She hoped there were so many surveillance feeds on Luna they couldn't possibly all be monitored.

Though they occasionally ventured up to the surface in
order to switch to a different shuttle line, they avoided it when
they could. Wolf warned them that most of the outer sectors
were manned by armed guards. Though they were meant to
be there for the security of the people, it seemed they spent

more time punishing anyone who dared to speak out against the crown. The few times they did sneak up into the surface domes, they managed to go unassaulted in their disguises and cowed postures, but Cinder knew it wouldn't be long before security measures were increased all over Luna.

They barely talked. Cinder spent the hours mulling over the battle in the docks, folding every misstep over in her head again and again, trying to determine a way she could have gotten them all away safely, trying to rescue Cress, trying to keep Kai out of Levana's clutches.

She never found a good solution.

The constant churning of her thoughts threatened to drive her mad.

The farther they traveled from Artemisia, the more their surroundings changed. It began to feel like they'd stepped into a different world altogether. Judging from how opulent the royal docks were, Cinder had constructed an image in her head of how beautiful all of Luna must be. But it soon became clear that the outer sectors received none of the capital's luxuries. Each platform they passed held new signs of neglect—crumbling stone walls and flickering lights. Graffiti scribbled onto the tunnel walls spoke of unrest.

SHE'S WATCHING . . . , read one message, painted in white upon the black cave walls. Another asked, **HAVE YOU SEEN MY SON?**

"How would we know if we had?" Iko asked. "They didn't leave a description."

"I think it's meant to be thought provoking," said Cinder.

Iko frowned, looking unprovoked.

They stopped when they heard a shuttle approaching or when they had to wait for a platform to clear, relishing their brief respites before moving on. They had brought a couple packs of food rations—not knowing when they would have an opportunity to find more—and Cinder doled them out in small increments, even though no one was all that hungry.

Though Cinder knew she couldn't be the only one whose back was sore and legs were aching, no one complained. Iko alone kept a graceful bounce to her step, having been fully charged before they left Kai's ship.

By shuttle, this trip should have lasted only a couple of hours. By the time they finally arrived at their destination, Cinder's internal clock told her they had left Artemisia over nineteen hours ago.

When they emerged from the darkened tunnel onto the shuttle platform of RM-9: REGOLITH MINING, the elaborate beauty of Artemisia felt like a distant dream. Gone were the glistening tiles and intricate statues, gone were the polished woods and glowing orbs. This platform was dark and cold and tasted of still, sterile air. Every surface was covered in a layer of dust, years of footprints pressed into it. Cinder brushed her hand across a wall and her fingers came away coated in gray.

"Regolith dust," said Wolf. "It covers everything out here."

Iko pressed both of her palms against one wall. When she pulled away, two handprints remained, perfect, yet lacking the normal creases of a human palm.

"Doesn't seem healthy," Thorne muttered.

"It's not." Wolf swiped at his nose, like the dust was tickling him. "It gets in your lungs. Regolith sickness is common."

Cinder clenched her teeth and added *unhealthy living and work conditions* to her long list of problems she was going to address when she was queen.

Iko smeared her dust-covered hands on her pants. "It feels abandoned."

"Everyone's working, either in the mines or the factories."

Cinder checked her internal clock, which she had synced with Lunar time before leaving the Rampion. "We have about eight minutes before the workday ends." She turned to Wolf. "We can wait here, or we can try to find your parents' house. What do you want to do?"

He looked conflicted as he peered up a set of narrow, uneven steps. "We should wait here. There aren't many reasons for people to be on the streets during work hours. We'd be too obvious." He gulped. "Besides, they might not be there. My parents might be dead."

He tried to say it with nonchalance, but he failed.

"All right," said Cinder, stealing back into the shadows of the tunnel. "How far are we from the factories?"

Wolf's brow was drawn, and she could see him straining to remember the details of his childhood home. "Not far. I remember them all being clustered near the dome's center. We should be able to blend in with the laborers as soon as the day ends."

"And the mines?"

"Those are farther away. There are two mine entrances on the other side of the dome. Regolith is one of the few natural resources Luna has, so it's a big industry."

"So . . . ," started Thorne, scratching his ear, "your best resource is . . . rocks?"

Wolf shrugged. "We have a lot of them."

"Not just rock," said Cinder, as her net database fed her an abundance of unsolicited information. "Regolith is full of metals and compounds too. Iron and magnesium in the highlands, aluminum and silica in the lowlands." She chewed the inside of her cheek. "I figured all of the metal would have had to come from Earth."

"A lot of it did, ages ago," said Wolf. "We've become experts at recycling the materials that were brought up from Earth during colonization. But we've also learned to make do. Most new construction uses materials mined from regolith—stone, metal, soil...Almost the entire city of Artemisia was built from regolith." He paused. "Well, and wood. We grow trees in the lumber sectors."

Cinder stopped listening. She had already educated herself as well as she could on Luna's resources and industries. Though, for their purposes, she'd spent most of her time researching Lunar media and transportation.

It was all controlled by the government, of course. Levana didn't want the outer sectors to have easy communication with one another. The less interaction her citizens had with each other, the more difficult it would be for them to form a rebellion.

A series of chimes pealed through the tunnel, making her jump. A short melody followed.

"The Lunar anthem," said Wolf, his expression dark, as if he had long harbored a deep hatred for the song.

The anthem was followed by a pleasant female voice: *"This workday has ended. Stamp your times and retire to your homes. We hope you enjoyed this workday and look forward to your return tomorrow."*

Thorne grunted. "How considerate."

Soon they could hear the drumming footsteps of exhausted workers pouring into the streets.

Wolf cocked his head, indicating it was time, and led them up the steps. They emerged into artificial daylight, where the dome's curved glass blocked out the glow of stars. This sector was not much of an improvement over the tunnels below. Cinder was staring at a patchwork of browns and grays. Narrow streets and run-down buildings that had no glass in their windows. And dust, dust, so much dust.

Cinder found herself shrinking away from the first sparse groups of people they saw—instinct telling her to stay hidden—but no one even glanced at them. The people they passed looked weary and filthy, hardly talking.

Wolf rolled his shoulders, his gaze darting over the buildings, the dust-covered streets, the artificial sky. Cinder wondered if he was embarrassed they were seeing this glimpse into his past, and she tried to imagine Wolf as a normal child, with parents who loved him and a home he grew up in. Before he was taken away and turned into a predator.

It was impossible to think that every member of Levana's army, every one of those mutants, had started out this way too. How many of them had been grateful to be given the chance to get away from these sectors with the dust that coated their homes and filled their lungs?

How many had been devastated to leave their families behind?

The graffiti echoed back at her: *Have you seen my son?*

Wolf pointed down one of the narrow streets. "This way. The residential streets are mostly in the outer rings of the sector."

They followed, trying to mimic the dragging feet and lowered heads of the laborers. It was difficult, when Cinder's own adrenaline was singing, her heartbeat starting to race.

The first part of her plan had already gone horribly wrong. She didn't know what she would do if this failed too. She needed Wolf's parents to be alive, to be allies. She needed the security they could offer—a safe place to hide while they figured out what they were going to do without Cress.

It was as far ahead as she could think.

Find a sanctuary.

Then she would start worrying about revolutions.

They hadn't gone far from the maglev tunnel when Cinder spotted the first guards, in full uniform, each clutching ominous guns in their arms. Unlike the civilians, their noses and mouths were covered to protect them from the dust.

Cinder shivered at the sight of them and cast her attention around, searching for the signature aura of a thaumaturge. She had never known a guard to be far from one, but she didn't sense any here.

How was it possible that a few weak-minded guards could hold such power over hundreds of gifted civilians? Though she guessed the Lunars in these outer sectors wouldn't be nearly as strong as Levana or her court, surely they could manipulate a few guards?

No sooner had she questioned it than the answer came to her.

These guards may not have a thaumaturge with them, but the threat was still there, implied in their very presence. The people of this sector could revolt. They could have these guards killed or enslaved easily. But such an act of defiance would bring the wrath of the queen down on them. The next guards that came would not be without the protection of a thaumaturge, and retribution would not be merciful.

When they passed by the guards, Cinder made sure to keep her face turned away.

They shuffled through the dome's center, where a water fountain stood in the middle of a dust-covered courtyard, forcing the crowd to flow around it. The fountain was carved into the figure of a woman, her head veiled and crowned, clear water pouring from her outspread hands as if she were offering life itself to the people who crossed her path.

The sight of it made the blood freeze in Cinder's veins. Levana had been queen for barely over a decade, yet she'd already put her mark on these far-reaching sectors.

Such a beautiful, serene fountain, but it felt like a threat.

They followed the dispersing crowd through blocks of factories and warehouses that smelled of chemicals, before the industrial buildings gave way to houses.

Though *houses* was a relative term. More like shacks, these homes were as unplanned and patched together as the overcrowded Phoenix Tower Apartments in New Beijing. Now Cinder understood what Wolf meant by how they had become experts at recycling materials. Every wall and roof looked like it had been cut and chopped and resoldered and rebolted and twisted and reconfigured again. As there was no weather to rust or corrode the materials, they were left to deteriorate at the hands of people. Houses pulled apart and reconstituted as families moved and changed and grew. The entire neighborhood was a ramshackle assortment of metal sheets and wood panels and stray materials left abandoned in the spaces between, waiting to be given a new use.

Wolf froze.

Nerves humming, Cinder scanned the nearby windows and opened the tip of her pointer finger in preparation for an attack. "What is it?"

Wolf didn't speak. Didn't move. He was focused on a house down the street, unblinking.

"Wolf?"

His breath rattled. "It might be nothing, but I think ... I thought I smelled my mother. A soap that seemed familiar ... though I didn't have these senses last time I saw her. It might not ..."

He looked burdened and afraid.

He also looked *hopeful.*

A few of the shanties had flower boxes hung from their windows, and some of them even had live flowers. The house Wolf was staring at was one of them—a messy cluster of blue daisies spilling over the rough-hewn wood. They were a spot of beauty, simple and elegant and completely at odds with their dreary surroundings.

They paused in front of the house. There was no yard, only a spot of concrete in front of a plain door. There was one window but it had no glass. Instead, faded fabric had been tacked around its frame.

Wolf was rooted to the ground, so it was Thorne who shouldered past him and gave a quick rap against the door.

With the fabric alone acting as a sound barrier, they could hear every creak of the floors within as someone came to the door and opened it a timid crack. A small woman peeked out, alarmed when she saw Thorne. She was naturally petite but unnaturally gaunt, as if she hadn't had a complete meal in years. Brown hair was chopped short, and though she had olive-toned skin like Wolf's, her eyes were coal black, nothing like his striking green.

Thorne flashed his most disarming smile.

It had no obvious effect.

"Mrs. Kesley?"

"Yes, sir," she said meekly, her gaze sweeping out to the others. She passed over Wolf first, then Cinder and Iko, before her eyes rounded, almost comically. She gasped and looked at Wolf again, but then her lips turned down with distrust.

"My name," Thorne said, with a respectful tilt of his head, "is Captain Carswell Thorne. I believe you may know—"

A strangled sound escaped the woman. Her shock and

suspicion multiplied by the second, warring against each other as she stared at her son. She pulled open the door the rest of the way and took one hesitant step forward.

Wolf had become a statue. Cinder could feel the anxiety rolling off him in waves.

"Ze'ev?" the woman whispered.

"Mom," he whispered back.

The uncertainty cleared from her eyes, replaced with tears. She clapped both hands over her mouth and took another step forward. Paused again. Then she strode the rest of the way and wrapped her arms around Wolf. Though he dwarfed her in every way, he looked suddenly small and fragile, hunching down to fit better into her embrace.

Wolf's mother pulled away far enough to cup his face in her hands. Taking in how handsome and mature he'd become, or maybe wondering about all the scars.

Cinder spotted a tattoo on her forearm, in the same place where Wolf had one marking him as a special operative. His mother's, though, was stamped simply RM-9. It reminded Cinder of how someone might mark their pet, to be returned home in case it got lost.

"Mom," Wolf said again, choking down his emotions. "Can we come inside?"

The woman raked her attention over the others, pausing briefly on Iko. Cinder wondered if she was confounded by Iko's lack of bioelectricity, but she didn't ask. "Of course."

With those simple words, she extracted herself from Wolf and ushered them inside.

They found themselves in a tiny room with a single rocking chair and a sofa, a seam ripped open to reveal yellow stuffing inside. A fist-size holograph node was stuck in the center of one wall and a squat table was pushed beneath it. There was a drinking glass full of more blue daisies.

One doorway led to a short hall where Cinder assumed there were bedrooms and the washroom. A second door offered a glimpse into an equally small kitchen, the shelves and counters overflowing with dishes.

It looked like it hadn't been dusted in a year. But then, so did the woman.

Wolf hunched in the room as if he no longer physically fit inside it, while his mother gripped the back of the chair.

"Everyone," said Wolf, "this is my mother, Maha Kesley. Mom—this is Iko and Thorne and . . . Cinder." He chewed on the words like he wanted to say more, and Cinder knew he was debating whether or not to tell his mom her *true* identity.

Cinder did her best to look friendly. "Thank you for welcoming us. I'm afraid we've put you into a lot of danger by coming here."

Maha stood a little straighter, still wary.

Thorne had his hands in his pockets, as if he was afraid to touch anything. "Will your husband be home soon?"

Maha stared at him.

"We don't want any surprises," Cinder added.

Maha pursed her lips. She looked at Wolf, and Cinder knew. Wolf tensed.

"I'm sorry, Ze'ev," said Maha. "He died four years ago. There was an accident. At the factory."

Wolf's expression gave away nothing. Slowly, his head bobbed with acceptance. He'd seemed more surprised to see his mother alive than to learn of his father's death.

"Are you hungry?" said Maha, burying her shock. "You were always hungry . . . before. But I suppose you were a growing boy then . . ."

The words hung between them, filled with a lost childhood, so many years.

Wolf smiled, but not enough to show his sharp canine teeth. "That hasn't changed much."

Maha looked relieved. She tucked a stray hair behind her ear and bustled toward the kitchen. "Make yourselves comfortable. I think I might have some crackers."

Twenty-Five

JACIN FELT HEAVY WITH DREAD AS HE ENTERED THE THRONE
room. The seats reserved for the members of the court were
empty. Only the queen sat on her throne, with Aimery at her
side. Not even their personal guards were with them, which
meant that whatever this meeting was about, Levana didn't
trust anyone to know of it.

Cress, he thought. She knew about Cress. He'd been hiding her
in his private quarters, keeping her safe like he'd promised Winter he would, but he knew it couldn't last forever.

How had Levana found out?

A screen had been brought into the room, a large flat
netscreen like the ones they used for two-dimensional Earthen
media, only this one was more elaborate than anything Jacin
had seen on Earth. It was set on an easel and framed in polished
silver, bands of roses and thorns surrounding the screen as if it
were a piece of art. The queen sparing no expense, as usual.

Queen Levana and Thaumaturge Park both wore dark expressions as Jacin came to a stop and clicked his heels together,

trying not to think of the last time he'd stood in this spot. When he was sure he would be killed, and Winter would have to watch.

"You summoned, My Queen?"

"I did," Levana drawled, running her fingers over the arm of her throne.

He held his breath, racking his brain for some way he could explain Cress's presence that didn't incriminate Winter.

"I have been thinking a great deal about our little dilemma," said the queen. "I desire to put my trust in you again, as I did when you were under Sybil's care, yet I haven't been able to convince myself that you serve *me*. Your queen. And not ..." She whisked her fingers through the air, and her beautiful face took on something akin to a snarl. "Your *princess*."

Jacin's jaw tensed. He waited. Waited for her to accuse him of sheltering a known traitor. Waited for his punishment to be declared.

But the queen seemed to be waiting too.

Finally he dipped his head. "All due respect, Your Majesty, my becoming Princess Winter's guard was your decision. Not mine."

She shot him a sultry look. "And how very upset you seemed about it." Sighing, Levana rose to her feet and walked behind Winter's usual chair. She smoothed her fingers along the top of the upholstery. "After much deliberation, I have devised a test of sorts. A mission to prove your loyalty once and for all. I think, with this mission completed, there will be no qualms about placing you back into the service of my head thaumaturge. Aimery is eager to have your skills under his command."

Aimery's eyes glinted. "Quite."

Jacin's brows knit together and it dawned on him slowly that this wasn't about Cress at all.

He would have felt relief, except, if it *wasn't* about Cress . . .

"I told you before of my promise to my husband, Winter's father," Levana continued. "I told him I would protect the child to the best of my ability. All these years, I have held to that promise. I have taken care of her and raised her as my own."

Though he tried, Jacin could not stifle a surge of rebellion at these words. She had raised Winter as her own? No. She tortured Winter by making her attend every trial and execution, though everyone knew how she hated them. She had handed Winter the knife that disfigured her beautiful face. She had mocked Winter relentlessly for what she saw as her mental "weaknesses," having no idea how strong Winter had to be to avoid the temptation of using her glamour, and how much willpower it had taken her to suppress it over the years.

A wry smile crept over Levana's bloodred lips. "You do not like when I speak of your darling princess."

"My queen may speak of whomever she pleases." The response was automatic and monotone. It would make no difference to try to deny he cared for Winter, not when every person in this palace had witnessed their childhood antics, their games, and their mischief.

He'd grown up beside Winter because their fathers were so close, despite how improper it was for a princess to be climbing trees and playing at sword fights with the son of a lowly guard. He remembered wanting to protect her even then, even before he knew how much she needed protecting. He also remembered trying to steal a kiss from her, once—only once—when he was ten and she was eight. She laughed and turned away, scolding him. *Don't be silly. We can't do that until we're married.*

No, his only defense was to pretend he didn't care that

everyone knew it. That their taunts didn't bother him. That every time Levana mentioned the princess, his blood didn't turn to ice. That he wasn't terrified Levana would use Winter against him.

Levana stepped off the raised platform. "She has been given the best tutors, the finest clothes, the most exotic of pets. When she makes a request of me, I have tried my best to see it done."

Though she paused, Jacin did not think she was expecting a response.

"Despite all this, she does not belong here. Her mind is too weak for her to ever be useful, and her refusal to hide those hideous scars has made her a laughingstock among the court. She is making a mockery of the crown and the royal family." She set her jaw. "I did not realize the extent of her disgrace until recently. Aimery offered his own hand in marriage to the girl. I could not have hoped for a better match for a child who has no royal blood." Her tone became snarling and Jacin felt her studying him again, but he'd recaptured control of himself. She would get no rise from him, not even on this topic.

"But, no," said the queen at last. "The child refuses even this generous offer. For no other reason, I can fathom, than to jilt my most worthy counselor and bring further humiliation on this court." She tilted her chin up. "Then there was the incident in AR-2. I trust you remember?"

His mouth turned sour. If he had not been so careful to hide his mounting dread, he would have cursed.

"No?" Levana purred when he said nothing. "Allow me to spark your memory."

Her fingers glided across the netscreen. It flickered to life inside its elaborate frame, showing footage of a quaint little row of shops. He saw himself, smiling at Winter. Nudging her with his shoulder, and letting her nudge him back. Their eyes taking glimpses of each other when the other wasn't looking.

His chest felt hollowed out. Anyone could see how they felt about each other.

Jacin watched, but he didn't have to. He remembered the children and their handmade crown of twigs. He remembered how beautiful Winter had looked as she put it on her head, unconcerned. He remembered ripping it away and stuffing it into the basket.

He had hoped the whole incident would go unnoticed.

He'd known better. Hope was a coward's tool.

His attention shifted back to the queen, but she was scowling at the imagery, loathing in her eyes. His gut churned. She had mentioned a special mission for him that would prove his loyalty, yet all she'd talked about was Winter and what an embarrassment she'd become.

"I'm disappointed in you, Sir Clay." Levana rounded on him. "I thought I could trust you to keep her under control, to make sure she didn't do anything to embarrass me and my court. But you failed. Did you think it was proper for her to go gallivanting around the city, playing at being a queen before her loyal subjects?"

Jacin held his ground, already resigning himself to death. She had brought him here to have him executed after all. He was grateful she had decided to spare Winter the sight.

"Well? You have nothing to say in your defense?"

"No, My Queen," he said, "but I hope you'll allow me to speak in *her* defense. The children gave her a gift as thanks for purchasing some flowers from the florist. They were confused—they didn't understand what it would suggest. The princess meant nothing by this."

"Confused?" Levana's gaze turned brittle. "The children were *confused?*" She cackled. "And how much confusion am I to tolerate? Am I to ignore the sickening way they idolize her? How they talk about her *beauty* and her *scars* as if they were a badge of honor, when they have no idea how weak she is! Her illness, her delusions. She would be crushed if she ever sat on a throne, but they don't see that. No—they think only of themselves and their pretty princess, giving no thought to all I've done to bring them security and structure and—" She spun away, her shoulders trembling. "Am I to wait until they put a real crown on her head?"

Horror filled up Jacin's chest and this time he couldn't disguise it.

She was psychotic.

This he'd known, of course. But he'd never seen her vanity and greed and envy enflame her like this. She'd become irrational, and her anger was directed at Winter.

No—Winter and *Selene.* That's where this was coming from. There was a girl claiming to be her lost niece and Levana felt threatened. She was worried that her grip on the throne was loosening and she was overcompensating with paranoia and tightening control.

Jacin placed a fist to his chest. "My Queen, I assure you the princess is not a threat to your crown."

"Would you not bow to her?" said Levana, spinning back to face him with venom in her eyes. "You, who love her so dutifully? Who are so loyal to the royal family?"

He forced down a gulp. "She is not of royal blood. She can never be queen."

"No. She *will* never be queen." She swayed toward him, and he felt like he was being encircled by a python, smothered and choked. "Because you are my loyal servant, as you have so vehemently proclaimed. And you are going to kill her."

Jacin's tongue ran dry as moon rock. "No," he whispered.

Levana raised an eyebrow.

"I mean—My Queen." He cleared his throat. "You can't . . ." He looked at Aimery, who was half smiling, pleased with this decision. "Please. Ask her to marry you again. I'll talk to her. I'll make sure she agrees. She can still be useful—it's a good match. She's just nervous—"

"You dare to question me?" said Levana.

His pulse thundered. "Please."

"I offered my hand to the princess as a kindness," said Aimery, "to protect her from the offers of far less sympathetic suitors. Her refusal has demonstrated how ungrateful she is. I would no longer take her if she begged me."

Jacin clenched his jaw. His heart was racing now and he couldn't stop it.

The queen's attention softened, full of honey and sugar. She was close to him. Close enough that he could grab his knife and cut her throat.

Would his arm be faster than her thoughts? Would it be faster than Aimery's?

"Dearest Sir Clay," she mused, and he wondered if she'd detected his desperation. "Do not think I am unaware of what I am asking you to do and how difficult it will be for you. But I am being *merciful.* I know you will be quick. She will not suffer at your hands. In this way, I also fulfill my promise to her father, don't you see?"

She was insane. Absolutely insane.

The worst of it was that he thought she might actually believe what she was saying.

His fingers twitched. A drop of sweat slipped down his neck.

"I can't," he said. "I won't. Please . . . please spare her. Take away her title. Turn her into a servant. Or banish her to the outer sectors, and you'll never hear from her again, I promise you . . ."

With a withering glare, Levana turned away and sighed. "How many lives would you sacrifice for hers?" She strolled toward the screen. The video was paused now, showing the three children in the doorway. "Would you rather I had these children killed instead?"

His heart kicked, trying to free itself from his rib cage.

"Or what about . . ." She turned back to him, tapping a finger against the corner of her mouth. "Your parents? If I recall correctly, Sir Garrison Clay was transferred to a guard post in one of the outer sectors. Tell me, when was the last time you spoke to them?"

He pressed his lips together, frightened that any admission could be turned against him. He had not seen or spoken to his parents in years. Just like with Winter, he had been sure the best way to protect his loved ones was to pretend he didn't love them at all, so they could never be used against him. Just as Levana was using them now.

How had he failed like this? He couldn't protect anyone. He couldn't save anyone—

He knew his face was contorted with panic, but he couldn't stifle it. He wanted to fall to his knees and plead for her to change her mind. He would do anything, *anything* but this.

"If you refuse me again," Levana said, "it will be clear that your loyalty is false. You will be executed for treason and your parents will follow. Then I will send Jerrico to deal with the princess, and I do not think he will be as gentle with her as you would have been."

Jacin choked back his misery. It would do him no good.

The thought of Jerrico—the smug and brutal captain of the guard—being given this same order made his blood run cold.

"Will you complete this task for me, Sir Clay?"

He bowed his head to hide his despair, though the show of respect nearly killed him.

"I will. My Queen."

Twenty-Six

FOR THE FIRST TIME SINCE SHE HAD ABANDONED IT, CRESS found herself missing her satellite. Jacin's private quarters were smaller than her satellite had been. The walls were so thin that she dared not even sing to pass the time. And when she needed to use the facilities, she had to wait for Jacin to get off his shift so he could sneak her in and out of the washroom that was shared between the guards and their families, all of whom lived in this underground wing of the palace. Once she crossed paths with another person, and while it was only a guard's wife who smiled kindly at her without any sign of suspicion, the encounter left Cress shaken.

She sensed the queen and her court all around her. She was aware at every moment that one person recognizing her for a shell would mean death. Perhaps torture and interrogation first. She was sick with anxiety for her own safety and terrified for the fate of her friends. She was frustrated that Jacin never had any news about them.

She told herself this was a good sign. Jacin would know if they'd been found. Wouldn't he?

Cress distracted herself doing what she could to help Cinder's cause with the limited resources available to her in Jacin's quarters. She still had her portscreen, and though she dared not send any comms, knowing how easily they could be traced, she was able to connect to the queen's broadcasting system via the holograph node embedded in Jacin's wall. The nodes were everywhere on Luna—as common as netscreens on Earth, and the feeds as easily hacked. She still had Cinder's prerecorded video stored in her port but she was afraid to do anything with it without knowing whether Cinder and the others were ready. Instead she spent her time interrupting propaganda messages from the queen and trying to come up with some way she could indicate to her friends that she was alive and relatively safe. She could never think of anything that wasn't either too obvious or too obscure though, and she was too timid to do anything that could alert the queen to her presence.

She wished again and again that she had access to the same technology she'd had in the satellite. She felt more cut off from the world than she ever had—with no media to view but that approved by the crown. No way to send a direct communication. No access to Luna's surveillance network or security systems and, hence, no way to fulfill the duties Cinder had given her. As the hours merged into days, she grew more anxious and addled, itching to get out of this enclosed space and *do* something.

She was altering the soundtrack from a royal message about their "brave victories against the weak-minded Earthens," when hard-soled footsteps in the hall made her pause.

They stopped outside Jacin's door. Cress disconnected her portscreen, threw herself off Jacin's cot, and scurried underneath it, pressing herself as close to the wall as possible. Outside, she heard the input of a code and fingerprint check on the lock. The door opened and shut.

Her heart thumped. "Wait."

"I've been waiting a long time to give this to you."

"Kai—"

With an expression as serious as politics, he pulled his hand from behind his back. In it was cupped a small metal foot, frayed wires sticking up from the cavity and the joints packed with grease.

Cinder released her breath, then started to laugh. "You—*ugh*."

"Are you terribly disappointed, because I'm sure Luna has some great jewelry stores if you wanted me to—"

"Shut up," she said, taking the foot. She turned it over in her palms, shaking her head. "I keep trying to get rid of this thing, but somehow it keeps finding its way back to me. What made you keep it?"

"It occurred to me that if I could find the cyborg that fit this foot, it must be a sign we were meant to be together." He twisted his lips to one side. "But then I realized it would probably fit an eight-year-old."

"Eleven, actually."

"Close enough." He hesitated. "Honestly, I guess it was the only thing I had to connect me to you when I thought I'd never see you again."

She slid her gaze off the foot. "Why are you still kneeling?"

Kai reached for her prosthetic hand and brushed his lips against her newly polished knuckles. "You'll have to get used to people kneeling to you. It kind of comes with the territory."

"I'm going to make it a law that the correct way to address your sovereign is by giving a high five."

Kai's smile brightened. "That's genius. Me too."

Cinder pulled her hand away from him and sat down, letting

her legs hang over the edge. Her thoughts grew serious again as she stared at the metal foot. "Actually, there's something I wanted to get your opinion on."

Kai settled beside her. His expression turned curious, and she looked away, bracing herself. "I think—" She stopped. Gulped. Started again. "I've decided to dissolve the Lunar monarchy."

Pressing her lips together, she waited. The silence became solid in the space between them. But Kai didn't ask "Why?" or "How?" or "Are you insane?"

Instead, he said, "When?"

"I don't know. When things have calmed down. When I think they can handle it." She took in a deep breath. "It will happen again. Some king or queen is going to brainwash the people, use their power to enslave them ... There has to be some division of power, some checks and balances ... so I've decided to change Luna into a republic, elected officials and all." She bit her lip. She still felt silly talking politics like she had a clue, and it wasn't until Kai nodded, thoughtful, that she realized how important his approval had been to her. She swallowed around the lump in her throat. "You think it's a good idea?"

"I think it will be difficult. People don't like change, and even the citizens who were oppressed under Levana immediately accepted you as their new queen. Plus, they have that whole superstition thing about the royal bloodline. But ... I think you're right. I think it's what Luna needs."

She felt as though an entire moon had been lifted off her shoulders.

"What will you do then? After you abdicate?"

"I don't know. I hear Thorne is looking for a full-time mechanic." She shrugged, but Kai went on looking pensive. "What?"

"I think you should come back to the Commonwealth. You

could stay in the palace, as a Lunar ambassador. It would be a show of good faith. Proof that Earth and Luna can work together, *coincide* together."

Cinder chewed on the inside of her cheek. "I thought the people of the Commonwealth hated me," she said. "For the kidnapping. And all that other stuff that happened."

"Please. You're the lost princess that saved them from the reign of *Empress* Levana. I heard there's a toy company that wants to make action figures of you. And they want to put up a statue where your booth used to be at the market."

She grimaced.

Chuckling, Kai took her hand. "Whenever you come back, you will be welcomed with open arms. And after everything that's happened, you're probably going to have about two hundred thousand guys wanting to take you to the Annual Peace Ball next year. I expect the offers to start rolling in any day now."

"I highly doubt that."

"Just wait, you'll see." He tilted his head, clumps of hair falling into his eyes. "I figured it couldn't hurt to get my name on the list before anyone else steals you away. If we start now, and plan frequent visits between Earth and Luna, I might even have time to teach you to dance."

Cinder bit her lip to disguise a budding smile.

"Please say yes," said Kai.

Fiddling with the dead wires of her old foot, she asked, "Do I have to wear a dress?"

"I don't care if you wear military boots and cargo pants."

"I just might."

"Good."

"Iko would kill me." She pretended to be considering it as she cast her gaze toward the sky. "Can I bring my friends?"

"I will personally extend invitations to the entire Rampion crew. We'll make a reunion out of it."

"Even Iko?"

"I'll find her a date."

"Because there's a rule against androids coming to the ball, you know."

"I think I know someone who can change that rule."

Grinning, she scooted a bit closer. The idea of going back to the ball and facing all those people who had stared at her with such horror and contempt filled her with copious amounts of everything from anxiety to dread to unspeakable joy.

"I would be honored," she said.

His eyes warmed. "And those dance lessons?"

"Don't press your luck."

Kai tilted her chin toward him and kissed her. She didn't know what number it was—she'd finally figured out how to turn off her brain's auto-count function and she didn't care how many times he kissed her. She did care that every kiss no longer felt like their last.

Except, when Kai pulled away, a hint of sadness had slipped into his expression. "Cinder, I believe you would make a great ruler. I believe this decision is proof of that." He hesitated. "But I also know you never wanted to be queen. Not really."

Cinder had never told him that, and she wondered if it had been obvious this whole time.

"But I have to ask if"—Kai hesitated—"if you think, *someday*, you might consider being an empress."

Cinder forced herself to hold his gaze, and to swallow the lighthearted joke that rose to the tip of her tongue. He wasn't teasing her about engagement rings and dance lessons. This was a real question, from a real emperor, who had the real future of his country to consider.

If she wanted to be a part of his future, she'd have to be a part of it all.

"I would consider it," she said, then took in the first full breath she'd taken in days. "Someday."

His grin returned, full force and full of relief.

He put an arm around her and Cinder couldn't smother her own smile as she leaned against him, staring at Artemisia Lake and the white city and planet Earth surrounded by stars. She spun the cumbersome, hateful foot in her fingers. Ever since she could remember, it had been a burden. A constant reminder that she was worthless, she was unimportant, she was nothing but a cyborg.

She held the foot over the water and let go.

And they all lived happily to the end of their days.

Acknowledgments

My heart overfloweth with gratitude . . .

For everyone at Macmillan Children's, including, but not limited to: Jean Feiwel, Liz Szabla, Jon Yaged, Nicole Banholzer, Molly Brouillette, Lauren Burniac, Mariel Dawson, Lucy Del Priore, Liz Fithian, Courtney Griffin, Angus Killick, Johanna Kirby, Anna Roberto, Caitlin Sweeny, Mary Van Akin, Allison Verost, Ksenia Winnicki, and countless more behind-the-scenes advocates for these books. You are all so brilliant and creative and I'm so lucky to be working with you. I also want to give special thanks to the cover designer, Rich Deas, and illustrator, Michael O, who together have created some of the most gorgeous book covers an author could hope for. Thanks also to my copyeditor, Anne Heausler, for your careful attention and surprisingly excellent knowledge of moon geology.

For Rebecca Soler, the ridiculously talented audiobook narrator, along with Samantha Edelson and the whole crew at Macmillan Audio for bringing these stories to life in such a lively and tangible way.

For my intrepid agent and her team: Jill Grinberg, Cheryl Pientka, Katelyn Detweiler, and Denise St. Pierre. Thank you for your constant faith, guidance, and zeal for toasting every milestone. (*Winter* is done—cheers!)

For my beta readers, Tamara Felsinger, Jennifer Johnson, and Meghan Stone-Burgess, who have been with me since the start of this crazy journey. Time and again you've forced me to dig deeper and push harder, and your invaluable feedback has made such a tremendous difference to this series and for me as a writer. Plus, I just really adore you all.

For the Sailor Moon fandom, from those who gave me courage back when I was a fledgling fanfiction writer, to some of my dearest friends who still make me laugh with your hijinks. (There, I put Jacin in a towel. *Are you happy??*)

We often talk about writing being a solitary profession, but it's hard to tell when you're surrounded by wonderful fellow writers as I've been. I'm grateful for my local partners-in-crime—Gennifer Albin (we miss you!), Martha Brockenbrough, Corry Lee, Lish McBride, Ayesha Patel, and Rori Shay—for keeping me inspired and focused during our many writing dates and retreats. I'm so glad to have met each of you. Thanks also to Mary Christine Weber and Jay Asher, who joined me for a super-fun interview in the *Cress* paperback, and to so many writers who have joked, inspired, commiserated, motivated, taught, toured with, and encouraged me throughout this epic book-writing quest: Anna Banks, Leigh Bardugo, Stephanie Bodeen, Jennifer Bosworth, Jessica Brody, Alexandra Coutts, Jennifer Ellision, Elizabeth Eulberg, Elizabeth Fama, Nikki Kelly, Robin LaFevers, Emmy Laybourne, Beth Revis, Leila Sales, and Jessica Spotswood, with sincere apologies to anyone I might have missed.

For the librarians, teachers, booksellers, and bloggers who've rallied around this series. From book talks to art assignments, staff picks to GoodReads reviews, your enthusiasm has introduced countless readers to the Lunar Chronicles and I am enormously grateful for all you've done.

For my friends and family, who plan launch parties, take photos, make dinners, babysit, pitch my books to random people at the supermarket, do my hair, make crowns, share book recommendations, help me shop for event outfits, and constantly remind me of the important things in life. Thank you; I love you.

For Jesse, who does so much so I can stay focused on writing and dreaming, dreaming and writing. I love you with my whole heart. And for Sarah and Emily, whose smiles have made this the brightest year of my life.

Lastly, I have infinite gratitude for the readers (yes, you!). Over the past years, you've made fanart and written letters, held in-depth discussions on the merits of various OTPs, shared with me your struggles and joys, hosted read-a-thons, donned costumes and red high heels, driven for hours to attend book signings, dreamed up movie fancastings, baked Lunar Chronicles cupcakes, started Tumblrs and compiled Pinterest boards, and so so so much more. This tale belongs to you now, as much as to me, and I couldn't feel as though I'm putting it in better hands. If you need me, I'll be thanking all the stars for each of you, one by one.

Thank you for reading this FEIWEL AND FRIENDS book.

The Friends who made

possible are:

Jean Feiwel
publisher

Liz Szabla
editor in chief

Rich Deas
senior creative director

Holly West
associate editor

Dave Barrett
executive managing editor

Nicole Liebowitz Moulaison
senior production manager

Anna Roberto
associate editor

Christine Barcellona
associate editor

Emily Settle
administrative assistant

Anna Poon
editorial assistant

Follow us on Facebook or visit us online at mackids.com.

OUR BOOKS ARE FRIENDS FOR LIFE